Specialist

KINGS OF THE EAST #12

CHARITY PARKERSON

PUNK & SISSY PUBLICATIONS

Copyright

THE SCANNING, UPLOADING, AND distributing of this book via the internet or via any other means without the permission of the copyright owner is illegal and punishable by law. Criminal copyright infringement, including infringement without monetary gain, is investigated by the FBI and is punishable by up to 5 years in federal prison and a fine of $250,000. Please purchase only authorized electronic editions, and do not take part in or encourage electronic piracy of copyrighted materials. Brief

—Warning: This book is intended for readers over the age of 18. Some of my books contain allusions to past abuse and trauma. I try to have nothing triggering on page and treat every situation with care.

Contents

Introduction	1
Author Note	3
Chapter One	4
Chapter Two	18
Chapter Three	49
Chapter Four	81
Chapter Five	93
Chapter Six	112
Chapter Seven	140
Chapter Eight	162

Chapter Nine   188

About the Author   203

Content   205

Introduction

*DANTE MAKES PROBLEMS AND **messes disappear for a crime family. Marshall is on the verge of landing on that list. Neither man has felt this alive before.***

As a rescue from one of Zander's team's missions, Dante has vowed to dedicate his life to the cause. It's a mission he took not only to reclaim his life, but as a way to stay close to the doctor who captured his heart the moment they met. Unfortunately, that man recently married someone else before Dante ever found the words to express his feelings. So he shows his affection another way: by protecting him from the man stalking his new husband

Marshall wouldn't say he was stalking anyone. He idolizes a life he'll never have. Marshall spent his best years focused on being a father. Now his daughter is grown, and it's fully hit him he's middle-aged and alone. Then this twenty-something troublemaker appeared in his life. Dante irritates him in an unexpected way. Marshall doesn't know why he can't shake him. All he knows is it can't be love.

Specialist is the twelfth book in Charity Parkerson's Kings of the East series where assassins, crime lords, and mafia bosses run the world. These books are best when read in order.

Author Note

THIS SERIES IS DARKER than my usual writing. If you need a list of potential triggers, you can skip to the end of this book and find a list after the About Author page. You can also visit my website at charityparkerson.com/kings-of-the-east, if you'd prefer.

Chapter One

IN A CROWDED RESTAURANT, in a neighborhood that catered to the gay community, Dante sat at a table in the corner and watched. Quiet observation was one of his strongest traits. He had an excellent attention to detail. As a biohazard specialist for Kapra Enterprises, Dante had to be a perfectionist. He couldn't miss a single detail or leave a solitary clue behind. It was his job to ensure the men who worked in elimination never got caught. Today, he worked in a self-appointed role that had nothing to do with his job.

Seven years ago, Zander Kapra's team of elite forces had rescued Dante from a sex-trafficking ring. Dante had been fourteen at the time. He had spent the last seven years working on himself and repaying that debt. No matter how much therapy he received or sessions he spent with a psychiatrist, there was one secret he kept from everyone. Dante was in love with his doctor. Dr. A. had once lived in Dante's shoes. He understood. Dante would never forget for as long as he lived the first time Corey had looked at him. He had seen something in Corey's eyes that Dante had never seen before that day: kindness. That moment lived with Dante twenty-four-seven. Unfortunately, Corey had never looked at Dante with more than friendship, and Dante had never wanted to fuck that up. Three months ago, Dante lost his chance to confess his feelings forever. Corey had married another. Now Dante did the only thing he could. He watched Corey's back. That was what brought him here.

Three tables over, Marshall Waverley sat alone. Dante watched his every move. From all his research and observations, Marshall seemed to be exactly who he presented himself to be: a forty-year-old single father who owned a pool-cleaning company. It was a lucrative business. He was a handsome guy. Dante imagined Marshall could have whoever he wanted. That was why Dante couldn't understand why Marshall hadn't listened to Dante's first warning and was here now, stalking Corey's husband. Dante really hoped the guy didn't make Dante have to kill him. It didn't matter how hot Marshall might be. No one hurt Corey. Dante would make him disappear first.

In the deepest recesses of his mind, Marshall had a guilty secret, one he would never share with anyone. There was the tiniest part of him that was relieved his daughter had decided to leave a few months early to get settled in her new town after recently graduating from high school. She would soon start college in California and needed to find a part-time job. It wasn't something he was proud of, by any means. The thing was, he was a middle-aged gay man who had given up the best years of his life so his daughter wouldn't be discriminated against. He saw her decision as a moment of freedom for himself.

Marshall missed her, of course. It was hard not seeing her all the time. Terry was his daughter. His baby. But Marshall had raised a smart, independent woman, and she hadn't let him down. She would thrive.

Of course, now that Marshall could begin the second half of his life, he didn't know where to start. He was tired of eating lunch alone. Marshall signed his receipt and added a tip. No one should be as good at sitting alone in a restaurant as he had become over the years. At one time, these one-man lunches felt like a power move. Today, Marshall just felt sad.

"Still stalking Rhett, I see."

Marshall blinked at the sudden appearance of the young twenty-something man who filled the seat across from him. He had only met Dante once. They had shared this exact conversation then too. At the time, he had—somewhat—been stalking Rhett Porter, a PE teacher and porn star who made everything about Marshall hot. This time, Dante's accusation didn't make sense.

"I'm having lunch. Well, I just had lunch. What are you talking about?" Even Marshall heard the confusion in his voice. Truthfully, he didn't even know why he entertained this. He should walk away without engaging, but it felt too good not being alone. Pathetic.

Light green eyes stared at him, as if searching for any lie in his words. Dante flipped his shaggy blond hair to one side. Hickeys covered his neck. He motioned over his shoulder. "Rhett. You're stalking him again."

Marshall's gaze shifted. Sure enough, Rhett sat at a table across the room with his son. Marshall's forehead furrowed. He hadn't even noticed Rhett before Dante pointed him out. "Huh. I didn't know he was here." Marshall's gaze moved back to Dante. "Honestly, it seems like you're the one stalking me."

Dante set his elbow on the table and propped up his chin with his fist. His gorgeous eyes, heavy with eyeliner, danced with laughter. "Funny."

He didn't have to explain himself. Marshall didn't know why he did. "We're gay men living in the same small town. It only makes sense for us to end up in the same places occasionally."

"Okay." Dante jumped to his feet. "Let's go."

Marshall only stood because he was headed out anyhow. The move had nothing to do with his inability to disobey the confidence in Dante's voice. "Where are we going?"

Dante didn't respond until they were outside. "Your truck. I know how to fix this."

"Fix what?" Marshall dug his keys from his pocket and hit the unlock button. He didn't know why he couldn't stop doing everything Dante told him to do.

Dante climbed into the passenger seat.

Even with confusion clouding his good sense, Marshall couldn't deny he was intrigued. Any change at all from his mundane life was a welcome one. Marshall slid behind the wheel.

"Get that air going."

At Dante's command, Marshall started the truck.

Dante turned his way. "I understand your issue now. You're horny. Once you've gotten over it, you'll realize you're not really that into my friend's husband, and you'll leave him alone."

"Get out." Marshall had heard enough. He honestly hadn't known Rhett had been inside that restaurant. Marshall was tired of this game. He didn't understand why Dante had appointed himself as Rhett's guardian, but Marshall hadn't done anything to warrant this harassment. Before he had known who Rhett was in real life, he had been a subscriber to Rhett's porn site. Yes, he had lusted after the guy. It was porn. That was the point. Yes, he had asked Rhett on a date when he realized they lived in the same town. But no, he had not known Rhett was at the same restaurant today. No man-child half his age would bully and berate him for simply existing. Marshall had already served his time of suffering for being a gay man.

Dante made a dismissive gesture. "There's no reason for the hostility. Seriously. I get it. Rhett is sexy, and he put himself out there on the internet. You just need this out of your system."

Marshall stared at Dante, wondering if he had a screw loose. "I'm serious. Get out."

"Don't worry. I'm about to fix everything." Dante shifted to his knees. "Keep a watch out."

"What?" Before the word fully died on his lips, Dante was across the truck's cab. He unzipped Marshall's jeans.

"Whoa. Wait. What the hell?"

There was nowhere to go. If he shoved Dante's head away, it would hit the steering wheel. Marshall didn't want to hurt him. Plus… maybe he was a little interested. Dante was strangely alluring. With his sexy painted eyes and soft blond hair, he screamed youth and vitality. Dante was bold and everything Marshall wished he had been in his twenties before he had missed his chance.

Then Marshall's dick was in Dante's mouth. Dante sucked. Marshall's erection grew and there was no chance he would argue. He fought the urge to close his eyes and savor the moment, but he could see Rhett through the window. His blond hair shimmered… like the man taking Marshall's dick down his throat. Marshall stared at Rhett and buried his fingers in the soft locks. All the times he had jacked off while picturing Rhett came to life now. He was so close, yet so far away from the reality of what he wanted.

Then, before he realized it, Marshall's gaze moved to his lap, and he knew it wasn't Rhett. It was Dante. Sleek muscles on a trim body. Shaggy-haired with a tattoo covering his solid bicep, he was beautiful. Dante squeezed his balls and sucked his cock like a fucking professional. All Marshall could do was breathe and take it. Dante sucked hard and bobbed faster. Marshall's breathing turned more ragged by the second. Pressure climbed and drove him crazy with the need to blow. He didn't understand how he ended up here, but Marshall desperately wanted the release Dante's hot mouth promised. Then his whole body jerked as pleasure exploded through him. Dante kept sucking, stealing Marshall's soul. Whimpers escaped Marshall without his control. He pushed against the floorboard, desperately trying to get deeper down Dante's throat. Then it was over.

Marshall's half hard and soaking wet dick was hanging out in the wind while he fought to catch his breath. He held the door handle in a death grip while breathless pants burst from him.

Dante opened the door like nothing happened. "You'll be good now. Leave Rhett alone."

While his throat tried swelling closed and reality sank in, Marshall watched Dante jump into a red Dodge Challenger, looking completely unaffected. The humiliation was slow to hit but still it came for him nonetheless. He was a forty-year-old man who was so fucking desperate for anyone to touch him, he hadn't even put up a fight. Dante didn't want him. Marshall didn't know why he had done what he had, but it had been a mistake. Now Marshall felt emptier than ever, and he very much feared he had a new obsession. He could cry.

SPECIALIST

Chapter Two

MARSHALL KNEW HE WAS a mess and his actions bordered on insane. He couldn't care about any of that shit. With thoughts of Dante haunting him, he hadn't slept at all last night. Marshall blatantly parked where the ice cream shop, bakery, and coffee shop were all within sight and waited. The encounter with Dante wouldn't let him go. Honestly, Marshall didn't know if he waited to see Dante again, or if he hoped Dante caught him stalking Rhett. Either way, he felt like a crazy person.

SPECIALIST

Dante had to be half his age, but the number of times Marshall had pictured Dante tossing his hair and revealing that hickey had Marshall losing his mind. Someone had sucked Dante's neck like he gave them pleasure beyond reason. God knew Dante had rocked Marshall's body. He was too old for this shit. What was wrong with him? Everything about the entire situation felt wrong. Marshall couldn't stop.

Rhett's blue Bronco pulled into the coffee shop parking lot. Marshall chewed the side of his nail as he watched Rhett get his son out of the backseat and head inside. He counted to ten and stepped out of his truck. Marshall didn't move fast. He hoped Dante would spring from the shadows and save him from himself. God knew he didn't want to humiliate himself like this. He just wanted to find Dante. Marshall needed Dante to explain why he had blown Marshall in that restaurant parking lot. He needed to hear Dante say anything at all about what happened. Otherwise, Marshall had allowed something incredibly irresponsible to happen to him. Fuck. He was dumb. This was the most psychotic thing he had ever done in his life. He thought his heart might explode. Yet Marshall's feet didn't stop moving, and before he knew what he would do, Marshall stood behind Rhett in line. Let the games begin.

"Have you ever liked someone you shouldn't?"

Dante felt a little unprofessional talking to his boss about something so goddamn dumb, but here they were. To make matters worse, Zander wasn't just Dante's boss. He was the man who ran the west coast mafia, footed the bill to save Dante from sex traffickers seven years ago, and was also just intimidating as hell for a plethora of reasons. Yet Dante always found himself talking about things he shouldn't with Zander. Probably because Zander had been him once upon a time.

Zander leaned back in his chair and eyed Dante. He looked untouchable behind his huge oak desk. But Zander never dismissed Dante, no matter how trivial the matter. Zander seemed to give Dante's question some real thought before answering. "No. I can't say that I have. Before I took over the family, wanting anyone would have gotten me killed. Afterward, I refused to live in shame of anything I wanted. Why? Is this about Corey?"

"No."

As much as Dante hated how Zander always saw right through him, in this case, Zander was wrong. Well, sort of mistaken. Dante's entire purpose for shadowing Marshall had started because of Corey. Someone had to look out for the clueless yet adorable doctor who cared for all the rescued children. At one time, making Corey see him as a grown man who wanted him more than life had been all Dante cared about. Then Corey had gotten married, and Dante had lost his chance. Still, he had shadowed Marshall's every move the last few months because of Corey. So Zander wasn't completely off base.

"Well, that's not the whole of it. There is this guy who I think was kind of stalking

Corey's husband before they got married... or maybe he wasn't. I don't know." Now that Dante brought up the subject, he felt a bit ridiculous. Dante did as he pleased these days. He had left behind the victim he had once been and embraced his power. Nowadays, Dante brought men to their knees with zero shame. He couldn't explain the dumbassery he currently experienced for any reason he could pinpoint.

Zander sat forward. "Give me his info. I'll make sure he isn't a problem."

A smile snapped to Dante's lips. "No. That's not what I meant. Never mind."

Zander's shoulders relaxed. A wicked smile stretched his lips and his light green eyes flashed with humor. "Ah. I see. You watched him a minute too long and now you're intrigued. That's exactly how I fell in love with Maverick."

"Really?" Dante was fascinated. Zander had an amazing marriage, but he never talked about himself. Dante was beyond curious how Maverick—a man with no ties to the mafia—had landed the king of all men sitting across from him.

Zander nodded. He looked like a man in love as his gaze seemed to turn inward. "He fought the Friday night fights at my casino. I would go every Friday just to see him. He won every match, but I swore he fought only for me." Zander stroked his bottom lip, looking lost in thought. His smile said it all. He hadn't lost an ounce of interest in Maverick. Zander shook his head and continued. "He would leave the cage and hold my stare every step of the way until he passed. I was fascinated. Even though we had never spoken, I felt like I knew him. Like he knew me. The first time we spoke, I finally understood why I couldn't shake him. He's my soul mate. I believe that to the bottom of my heart. I think you just know."

That was a bit far. Dante was just a little more interested than usual. "It's not..." Dante's phone buzzed in his pocket. "Excuse me." Dante checked the device. He had a text from Rhett.

Rhett: *Random as hell, I know. I'm at the coffee shop with Rhorey and I ran into this guy I know, Marshall. He's asking for your number. I didn't know you two knew each other. What should I do?*

A smile that felt evil pulled at Dante's lips. He quickly responded.

Dante: *It's fine. Give it to him.*

Rhett: *Okay.*

Dante flashed Zander a smile. "Sorry to cut this short, but I need to take this."

A knowing look passed over Zander's features. "Of course. You know where to find me if you'd like to continue this conversation later."

"Thank you." Dante stood and headed for the door. Outside Zander's office, Dante made it to the elevator before his phone rang. Dante let it ring five times before he answered. He wouldn't look desperate. "Hello?"

"Hey. It's Marshall."

Dante smirked at Marshall's nervous tone. "I figured, since I just got the strangest text from Rhett. You really can't stay away from the guy, can you?"

"It's not like that."

The elevator opened, and Dante stepped inside. "What is it like, then?" He pushed the button for the twentieth floor and headed down to his room inside the Luna Hotel. Zander owned all the locations on the west coast. Since Dante's job required him to be wherever he was needed, Zander kept Dante a room at every location.

Marshall hummed. It was an uncomfortable sound. "I was wondering if we could meet for lunch."

"I'm working in California today."

"Oh." The disappointment in Marshall's voice was palpable. "What do you do?"

Dante shouldn't care. He didn't know why he, too, wanted to get together again. "I'll be back in town in the morning," he said, ignoring Marshall's question. "I could meet you somewhere then."

"Great. Yeah. Let me check my appointments real quick. I need to make sure I haven't been scheduled for anything."

Dante held his breath and counted to five. "Hold on. I'm getting a text." Dante stared at nothing and waited for the elevator door to open, dropping him off right outside his room. After he let himself into his room, he set Marshall free from waiting. "It looks like I'm needed back in Florida this afternoon. It's a six-hour flight and about a two-hour job. How about we meet at Lancaster's Bar on Ocean Way at ten tonight? It's quiet and stays open pretty late. We should have no problem talking there."

"I can do that."

Even though Marshall couldn't see him, Dante gave a sharp nod. There was no sense in waiting until tomorrow for what Marshall wanted. Marshall wasn't the first to come back for more. He wouldn't be the last. Dante had time. "Good. I'll see you then."

"Okay. Yeah. See you then."

As Dante disconnected their call, a smirk pulled at his lips. He hadn't planned to head back to Florida anytime soon. Since Corey got married, Dante stayed away more often all the time, even though he had recently rented a house there. But if Marshall couldn't stay away, then Dante would humor him. Maybe Dante had some daddy issues he needed to work out anyhow. Marshall looked like a good choice for the job.

Lancaster's Bar was a dark, too quiet hole in the wall that played soft jazz and smelled like whiskey. Marshall couldn't stop wiping his sweaty palms on his thighs as he waited for Dante. He had a bad habit of always being ridiculously early. Tonight was no exception. He used the time he had to kill by choosing a table in the corner where he could keep an eye on the door. They had the tall tables with the barstools that made it easy to see everything. His gaze moved over the room, taking in the ambience. Men sat close to each other, talking and openly flirting. He witnessed more than one stolen kiss and lingering embrace. The place made him long for someone to touch him. He wondered if that was why Dante chose this bar as a meeting spot. Dante seemed to possess an uncanny ability to read people. Maybe this was psychological torture for him approaching Rhett again. Or maybe Marshall overthought the entire situation. He no longer knew anything. Dante had obviously broken his brain with that blowjob. Marshall didn't know which way was up any longer.

"The corner table is always a smart choice."

Marshall blinked. Even while watching for him, Dante had gotten the drop on him. "Hey."

Dante snagged the stool on the other side of the tiny round table from him and sat. "Hey, yourself."

Marshall couldn't stop eyeing Dante's every feature. He looked like he should be in a band that played local dives on the weekends. Marshall wondered if he had any hidden piercings. "You look amazingly well rested for someone who's been across the county and worked today." Marshall imagined that was on youth, but still. He should look at least a little jetlagged.

Dante shrugged. "I'm used to it. My job has headquarters on both coasts, and I go where they tell me. I had a quick thing here tonight, but I might be in Prague tomorrow."

That was impressive for someone so young. "What do you do?"

"I'm a biohazard specialist for an international company."

"Like crime scene cleanup?" Even Marshall heard the confusion in his voice. He didn't know people had to travel for that.

Dante smiled. It was slow and sexy—like Marshall amused him. "Something like that. Why did you want to meet?"

Marshall rolled his beer bottle between his hands. His stomach fluttered. He felt like he was twelve and didn't know how to ask the questions he should. "I guess

I just wanted to know why you did what you did yesterday."

Laughter danced in Dante's eyes as if he found Marshall's question hilarious. "Because I felt like it, and—like I said yesterday—it's what you needed to move on from your obsession with Rhett."

There was more to it. There had to be. Marshall felt it in his gut... or maybe he was desperate to believe there was more. He rolled the bottle between his hands again. Marshall didn't know how to get more info from Dante. He was too out of practice.

Dante's smile never dimmed. He shook his head. "Seriously, Marsh. It was just a blowjob. I learned how to do that before I was five. It meant nothing."

It was like getting punched in the chest. Marshall forgot to be nervous. "Before you were five? What the fuck?" What sort of hell had Dante suffered?

Dante's smile tightened. "It meant nothing. Don't overthink things." He glanced around, looking uncomfortable and ready to disappear again. Marshall couldn't let that happen.

"Don't run." Even to his ears, Marshall's demand sounded soft and pleading.

Sexy eyes shaded with eyeliner shifted his way again and held his stare. "Do you want to go dancing with me? I just joined this local club that Rhett suggested. You should come with me. I'm in the mood to dance."

It was a work night and Marshall was forty, but he knew Dante would go even if he didn't. Oddly, Marshall hated the idea of Dante dancing with someone else. That meant he had to set aside the horrible confession Dante had dropped on him. "Sure."

A smile exploded across Dante's lips. "Good boy. I'll drive."

Marshall turned up his beer and finished it before following Dante to the door. His gaze automatically lowered to inspect Dante's body. He wore dark jeans. One leg was haphazardly tucked into a black work boot, as if he had put his shoes on in a rush or didn't care about his appearance. His white tank top molded his skin, showing the sleek muscles beneath. He was too skinny, like he was always on the move or never ate, but his body looked like he worked hard. Dante moved with such confidence, he made Marshall want to be seen with him.

When they reached Dante's red Challenger, the lights flashed. Dante opened the passenger side door for him. Marshall realized his nails were painted black. Marshall slid into the passenger seat and tried to act as if men opened car doors for him all the time. Dante winked as he closed the door. Marshall drew a steadying breath and released it slowly as he watched Dante circle the car. Leather and cologne filled his nostrils. Dante jumped behind the wheel and the car roared to life. They were off before Marshall put on his seatbelt. As he buckled in, he realized Dante hadn't.

"You should wear your seatbelt."

Dante tossed a laughing glance his way. "Yes, daddy."

Marshall didn't let it go because he was a father. "Seriously. I'm sure there's someone out there who would be devastated if anything happened to you."

Dante switched lanes. "I assure you there isn't."

"I would be." The quietly spoken words were out there before Marshall could call them back.

Dante didn't look his way again, but he put on his seatbelt. Marshall took it as a win. They pulled into the parking lot of a nondescript building. Marshall eyed the place.

"This is a club?" While there were a lot of cars in the parking lot, there was nothing about the outside that gave away the building as a nightclub.

Dante flashed him a secretive-looking grin. "Yep." He jumped from the car.

Marshall opened his door and Dante rushed to pull it the rest of the way open and shut it behind him. Dante headed for a metal door on the side of the building. There was an electronic fin-gerprint scanner next to the door. Dante scanned his fingerprint and opened the door. Music poured out as Dante waved Marshall ahead of him. Marshall tried not to wring his hands as he stepped inside. He hadn't been in a nightclub in ages.

They headed down a hallway together toward the flashing lights and music. As they stepped through the mouth of the hallway, Marshall froze. Half-dressed men thrusted against one another. There was a guy five feet away get-ting blown while sitting on a barstool at the bar. Marshall looked away. His gaze landed on another couple fucking against the wall. Marshall turned, ready to run before his mind realized what he had done.

Dante snagged his waist and walked him backward onto the dance floor. "Nope.

No thinking tonight. It's time to have fun."

In a matter of seconds, Marshall was in Dante's arms, with Dante grinding against him. Marshall's body moved without his mind guiding it. He was too transfixed by Dante to think straight.

"You brought me to a fetish club."

Dante kissed his neck. His tongue shot out, stroking Marshall's skin. "So? I also blew you in a parking lot where anyone could've seen." Dante grabbed Marshall's ass and squeezed. "I don't think your morals are as high as you're pretending right now."

Marshall sucked in a deep breath, fighting the lust that completely owned him with the simplest of touches from Dante. He had never met anyone as sexual as Dante, and it was overwhelming.

Marshall didn't know how to fight it, and he didn't think he wanted to.

"I don't understand what you want from me."

A wicked-sounding chuckle caressed the shell of his ear. "Yes. You do."

Frustration welled inside Marshall. Dante made him feel out of control. He wasn't much older than Marshall's daughter. Dante had dropped a huge fucked-up bombshell about his past on Marshall earlier. Marshall should be the adult and put a stop to this. If Dante had daddy issues, Marshall wanted no part of that. Dante needed help he couldn't give. Then Dante grabbed his throat, holding him in place while his mouth claimed Marshall's. The world disappeared. Marshall stopped trying to follow the music. He couldn't hear it anyway. His pulse pounded in his ears.

Marshall hadn't been a monk over the years. There was a guy he called when the celibacy became too much. This was different. Dante would burn him to the ground, then wipe his feet in the ash. This wasn't just sexual. Marshall no longer possessed an ounce of good sense. Dante used him, and Marshall took it. He was consumed by someone who had all his alarm bells clanging. Dante was dangerous. Marshall might not survive.

"Come to the bathroom with me."

Marshall didn't think he could do that. "I have a house with a bed. Come home with me."

Dante nipped Marshall's bottom lip, making him gasp. "I didn't ask for a counteroffer. Come to the bathroom with me."

He had to put a stop to this. Things were out of control. "No. I'm too old for that bullshit."

"That's too bad. I'm not."

Reality slapped Marshall in the face. Dante was right. He wasn't. Not only should Dante get to have all the fun Marshall missed when he became a dad, Dante offered to give Marshall the experiences he missed. Yet Marshall was still being the boring guy who had settled down too young. He already had regrets about everything he had missed over the years. Marshall didn't want more.

Without another thought, Marshall took Dante's hand and weaved through the crowd, following the overhead signs to the restroom. He was still nervous and thought this was a bad idea, but that wouldn't stop him. For whatever reason, Dante wanted him. Marshall would take this no-strings night and cherish it for the gift it was. Dante was an adult and he had chosen Marshall. Marshall might never get this chance again. He would take it.

Marshall made Dante proud as hell. He was catching on and learning how to let go. Life wasn't as serious as Marshall made it out to be. Neither of them were getting out alive, and when they were gone, no one would care what they had done. Everything they did on this earth was literally a forgotten memory waiting to happen. They may as well enjoy the ride.

Dante didn't meet anyone's stare as he hauled Marshall into a stall inside the bathroom. He could have fucked Marshall on the dance floor in a place like this, but Marshall might have walked away then. The bathroom was already a stretch for Marshall. Marshall still held some morals. Dante never had any such bullshit weighing him down.

The moment they were out of sight, Dante claimed Marshall's mouth. He sucked Marshall's tongue while he tugged at Marshall's clothes. Marshall was hard for him already. Dante laughed as the power rose inside him. He loved making men crave him. Dante had come into his power as an adult. Now he used it as often as possible.

"Admit it. You prepped for tonight, didn't you? You met me, ready to get fucked."

A pant escaped Marshall as Dante stroked his cock. "Yes."

Wicked satisfaction roared through Dante. "You're such a good boy. Now turn around and spread those cheeks. I'll make you fly."

The desperation in Marshall's eyes called to something deep inside Dante. Dante had watched him for too long. Followed him, trying to keep Corey safe. Dante had recognized something in Marshall. He knew what it was like to want someone he couldn't have. Dante had fucked hundreds of men, trying to fill a hole inside himself where he had always wanted Corey to be. Marshall touched no one despite the loneliness in his eyes. Dante could fill him. He could give Marshall back the years he had lost while playing the good parent.

Dante pulled out his wallet and found a condom and foil packet of lube. He didn't make Marshall wait. Dante knew Marshall might lose his nerve if he didn't keep Marshall burning for more. He quickly suited up and then ripped open the lube. Dante toyed with Marshall's asshole. Marshall moaned. The sound reverberated from the walls of the stall, mixing with the sounds coming from the stalls on either side of them. They weren't the only ones seeking release. Dante stretched Marshall. Marshall flattened his hands against the wall and pressed backward, silently begging for more. He was greedy and responsive. Dante told himself he just wanted to get off. He didn't care about Marshall. This was just sex.

Dante led his dick to Marshall's asshole. The tight ring of muscles resisted him before giving way. Marshall's body tried sucking him deeper. Dante closed his eyes and thrust. He held Marshall's hips while he lost himself to the sensation of heat surrounding his cock. Marshall became just another body to soothe his addiction. Sex gave Dante a rush of power like nothing else did. He was in control. Dante could get out and walk away right then, leaving Marshall to writhe in desperation. He made the rules now. No one used him.

Marshall whimpered and squirmed, trying to reach a goal only Dante could give him. Dante let it go on for a minute before changing angles and pounding the spot Marshall wanted. Cries of pleasure filled Dante's ears. He thrust faster and harder, focusing on the growing pressure. It didn't matter who was on his dick. Dante just wanted the rush.

"That's it, sexy. Let me hear your pleasure. Let everyone in this bathroom know I own this ass."

A loud cry tore from Marshall. His asshole squeezed Dante's cock before convulsing. Dante threw his head back and strained toward the edge. Then air burst from his lungs in a whoosh as ecstasy rocked his soul. Nothing mattered but the oblivion. Everything inside his mind went quiet as his dick twitched and spit inside Marshall's ass. He forgot who he was and why he existed. Dante clung to the peace. He already needed more.

Chapter Three

THE SUN FELT HOTTER than usual. Everything hurt. It had been years since Marshall felt like life kicked his ass, and he wanted to sleep for days. Every second of the night had been worth it. Flashes of Dante kissing and biting kept flaring to life in Marshall's head, making his body burn from more than the Florida heat.

"You look like shit. Are you getting sick too?"

Marshall winced at Beau's words. He didn't doubt he looked as bad as he felt. "Nah. It was just a long night." Marshall went back to pushing the vacuum across the pool's bottom. He hadn't expected Jay to call in today, but this was part of the job. Marshall might be the owner of his pool cleaning company, but he was no better than his employees. If there was no one else available to do a job, it was on him.

Beau nodded. His dark hair ruffled in the breeze. "Okay. Just making sure. You know there's a bad bout of the flu going around. Anyhow, I'm here to take over."

Marshall nodded and handed the vacuum off to Beau. He was more than happy to get out of the sun. "It's all yours." With a final wave, Marshall headed for his work truck and fired the air to full blast the second he could. He didn't waste any time before pointing the truck toward the office. He needed to drop off the vehicle and pick up his personal truck. Then he would grab some lunch and head home. Damn, he couldn't wait to go back to sleep. He couldn't remember the last time he was this tired. Thank God for Beau being amazing at his job. Otherwise, Marshall might have been stuck working in the sun all day.

Once inside his personal truck, Marshall didn't move. His arms felt heavy. He spaced out for a moment before shaking his head. His gaze landed on a shirt in his passenger seat. Images flashed through his head. Heated kisses that took his breath owned Marshall's thoughts. He could still taste Dante. Dante had taken him back to his truck and then climbed inside to suck Marshall's dick again. Damn. Every time he had thought he couldn't get hard again, Dante found a way. After pumping Dante's mouth full of cum, Dante had convinced Marshall to follow him home. He had left his shirt behind, looking sexy and tempting as sin as he had made his way to his car. Marshall chewed the side of his nail, picturing every delicious second. It turned out Dante had all the piercings Marshall had expected him to have. They were all equally hot as hell.

Without thinking, Marshall snagged the shirt and brought it to his nose. Fuck. It smelled just like him. Marshall's stomach muscles clenched. Before he knew what he would do next, Marshall was headed for Dante's place. If he wasn't home, Marshall would leave the shirt on his doorknob and go. Even if he was home, Marshall would simply give him the shirt. He wouldn't press his company on Dante. Marshall just wanted to see him. If only for a moment, Marshall wanted to see his wicked smile and bask in the knowledge he had won Dante for a moment out of time. For one night, this incredibly sexy guy had wanted him. Marshall needed to be near him.

He didn't have time to talk himself out of going before Marshall entered Dante's neighborhood. As he had been last night, Marshall was impressed by Dante. Marshall still didn't know how old Dante was, but he did well for himself. His house wasn't massive, like a few others nearby, but his neighborhood was upscale. Marshall had several clients in the area. It was obvious Dante made decent money at his profession for someone so young. There was a lot about Dante to like. Marshall still didn't understand how he had caught Dante's eye. It didn't truly matter, though. This was just Marshall enjoying life after years of being responsible. That didn't mean Dante didn't impress him. He did. One day, Dante would be some man's prized catch. Until then, Marshall would take what he could get. If that meant he only got last night, then so be it.

At Dante's place, Marshall took a deep breath for courage before grabbing Dante's shirt and heading for the door. If Dante was home, his car was in the garage, because Marshall didn't see it. If he wasn't home, Marshall might keep the shirt for a little longer. He wasn't quite ready to give up his only connection. As he reached the door, a breeze rushed over his skin. The hair stood on the back of his neck. Dante's front door creaked open a hair. Marshall's steps slowed. He tucked Dante's shirt into his back pocket and reached for the gun clipped to his belt. Marshall had been licensed to carry for fifteen years and did so every day after getting mugged trying to make a deposit for his business years ago. He had lost twenty grand that night, but he had gained a new rage. Marshall would never be a victim again.

The door rocked with the wind again. It never occurred to him to call the police. He was too focused on Dante. If Dante was in trouble, Marshall had to help. Air filled his lungs and steadied his nerves. Marshall pushed open the door and burst inside.

"Oh, good. You've come to put me out of my misery."

With his gun held in front of him, Marshall's gaze skimmed the room as his eyes adjusted from the bright sunlight to the darkened living room. Dante was stretched out on the couch nude. His skin was bright red, and his eyes looked feverish. Marshall quickly shoved his gun back into its holster.

"Jesus. I'm sorry. Your door wasn't latched, and I thought you might be in danger. What's wrong?"

"Flu."

That one word sounded as if it tore at Dante's throat. Marshall's heart squeezed in his chest. Dante looked like hell. Sweat covered his skin. A blanket on the floor looked as if it had been discarded in a fit. Clothes were scattered throughout the sparse living room. Dante's house was nice, but he barely owned any furniture.

"How can I help? Do you need me to take you to the doctor?"

Dante made a dismissive gesture. "Corey called me in some meds to shorten the length of the virus, but I don't feel good enough to go to the pharmacy. I've chosen death."

Marshall fought a smile at Dante's dramatics. "Come on, gorgeous. Let me help you to bed. Then you can make a list of what you need and tell me the name of your pharmacy. I'll take care of everything."

Gorgeous eyes feverish with misery stared at Marshall, but Dante didn't budge. "You should leave before you catch this."

"Babe, I raised a kid to adulthood. I'm pretty sure you could spit Ebola in my eye, and I'd be immune. So let's go."

Marshall helped Dante to his feet. He leaned on Marshall to the point Marshall more carried him than led him to the bedroom. By the time he had Dante tucked beneath the covers, Dante's teeth chattered. Worry ate at him. Despite taking care of his daughter during every childhood illness, Dante didn't look so good.

"Did you say your doctor is Corey, as in Rhett's husband?"

Dante answered through clenched teeth, as if trying to stop them from rattling from his head. "Don't get any ideas about using this as an excuse to stalk your favorite crush."

Marshall's eye roll was completely out of his control. "I'm here with you, worrying about you. I think maybe Corey needs to see you. Not just call you in a script."

Dante shook his head. "Don't worry about me. I just need some sleep. Corey doesn't need this virus in his house. Rhorey still isn't strong enough to withstand getting this sick."

Marshall sat on the bed at Dante's side. He rubbed Dante's stomach, trying to soothe him. "What's wrong with Rhorey?"

A sigh escaped Dante, as if he soaked up Marshall's affection. His eyes closed. "Everything. He should've died, but Corey saved him. Well, honestly, Rhett kept him alive with his willpower alone." Dante sounded out of his head. Marshall barely followed the conversation. Dante's voice got weaker by the second, while Marshall kept trying to soothe him into sleep. "Lucky kid. He has no idea how much they saved him. Not everyone gets lucky like that."

The backs of Marshall's eyes stung unexpectedly. He didn't understand why. There was just something in Dante's voice. It was pain and jealousy, like he had lost something he could never get back, and Marshall didn't think it was his childhood. Marshall wanted to fix him. "I'll take care of you. It's okay to sleep. Which pharmacy has your prescription?"

"Baker's," Dante mumbled.

Luckily, Marshall knew exactly what Dante meant. Baker's Pharmacy was a locally owned pharmacy that still sold counter-style milkshakes while people waited for their meds. Marshall waited until he knew Dante was out before leaving him alone. First, he checked Dante's kitchen. It was all granite and stainless steel. Everything was spotless. The cabinets were bare. Next, he checked the fridge, but it too was empty except for a few energy drinks. Marshall shook his head. As he headed for the door, it occurred to him he didn't even know Dante's last name or birthdate. Without that information, he couldn't pick up Dante's prescription.

SPECIALIST

He found Dante's wallet on the end table next to the couch. Marshall flipped it open, determined to only get the info he needed and move along. Instead, Marshall stared at the image on Dante's license. He looked so young. In fact, he was. Dante was only twenty-one. He had an October birthday. Halloween, actually. His license had been issued in California. Dante Wrath. It was the most metal name ever and sounded fake as hell. A matching social security card, credit card, and biohazard specialist certification ID said otherwise. Marshall had never wanted to know someone's story as badly. Dante Wrath fascinated the fuck out of Marshall.

Marshall set Dante's wallet aside. As he did, the cellphone next to it vibrated and the face lit. Marshall automatically focused on it. He didn't mean to snoop,

but he read the message without thinking.

Wulf: *1842 Sharpshooter Lane.*

Marshall flipped the phone over and
headed for the door. Hopefully, Dante
would wake up at some point and respond to the message. For now, Dante
needed to sleep, and Marshall had to get
moving. Dante needed him.

The last time Dante had felt this out of
his head was a time he didn't care to
remember. The room spun every time
he opened his eyes. He had made his
way to the bathroom twice by himself,
but that was about it. There was a small
part of him that was aware Marshall
was there, but Dante couldn't stay awake

long enough to hold on to a concept of time. Marshall fed him soup, made him drink water, and forced meds down his throat. Sometimes his skin could fry an egg, while other times, he shook to his nonexistent soul from the freezing temps. Nothing made sense.

Occasionally, Marshall would sit with him and rub his chest and stomach. He would keep Dante talking until sleep carried him away again. Dante had no clue what he said or what they talked about, but he recalled every second Marshall touched his skin. No one took care of Dante. Never had. Zander had rescued Dante and given him a new life, but that fresh start hadn't come with a loving family. Dante had been rebuilt into an independent man with a steady career. His mental health had been a top priority, but no one had shown him true affection. Not like Rhorey had gotten from Corey and Rhett. Dante had gotten to pick his name and profession. He had gotten to move on from being just a number, but then again—sometimes—he felt like he was still just a plaything, but in a different way. He was a cog in a machine with no real connections to anyone. If Marshall hadn't shown up out of the blue, maybe Dante would have simply died. He would have passed on with no one any wiser because there was no one. No one would check on him or care. No one would mourn.

Dante blinked at his darkened bedroom. The room didn't spin as much tonight. The house seemed eerily quiet, making Dante wonder if Marshall left. After a moment of gathering his bearings, Dante forced himself to roll upward. With his feet on the floor, Dante struggled for air as the room betrayed him and whirled around him. Dante locked his jaw and powered through, forcing his weak legs to work. He stood. After a moment, the floor stopped moving beneath his feet. Dante shuffled toward the living room. The floor lamp in the corner cast a soft glow throughout the room. Marshall had one arm across his eyes while stretched out on the couch. For a moment, Dante stared at him, wondering if he was dead. He seemed unnaturally still. When he saw Marshall's chest rise and fall, a wave of relief washed through him. Dante leaned against the wall in the mouth of the hallway. He didn't think he could make it back to bed. His legs were too weak.

A scraping noise cut through Dante's blurry mind, snapping his focus to the front door. The sound came again. Dante's gaze shot around the room. Marshall's gun was in its holster on the end table next to Dante's cellphone. Dante grabbed it and quickly pulled it from its holster. With both hands steadying the weapon, Dante kept it pointed at the door. He watched the handle turn and took a breath. It didn't matter he didn't feel good enough to clean up a crime scene tonight. He would kill whoever came through the door. Dante would never be a victim again. The door creeped open, and Dante's finger moved to the trigger. Wulf stuck his head inside and quickly hit the floor when he spotted the gun pointed at him.

Dante's shoulders fell. "Goddamn it, Wulf. I almost blew your fucking head off, dumbass."

Marshall shot from the couch and snagged the gun in one hand before catching Dante with the other. He tossed the gun aside as Dante's knees gave out.

Dante heard Wulf apologizing and explaining himself, but he only partially understood. It seemed he hadn't been answering his phone or showing up for work and Wulf had been worried. In a small way, Dante was touched. Mostly, he was too sick to care about anything at all. His nonexistent energy had been sent into the negative by the adrenaline rush. Marshall swept Dante into his arms and carried him back to bed. He didn't look the least bit frazzled by the experience.

"What are you doing up? I told you to shout if you needed anything."

"I don't remember any of that." He really didn't.

Wulf was on their heels. "What's going on, Dante? You can't just blow off Zander. I thought you were dead or something."

"He has the flu," Marshall snapped over his shoulder, making Dante smile.

"No one snaps at Wulf. That's funny." Dante felt almost delirious.

Marshall tucked Dante back into bed with a deep line between his eyebrows. He angrily tugged at the blankets. "I'll snap all I fucking want. I haven't spent the past two days trying to make you better for some dude to break in and lecture people."

"Seriously, man. I'm sorry. I thought Dante was in trouble or had finally offed himself. It's not like him to blow off work."

Marshall straightened and glared at Wulf.

Wulf looked like a nervous teenager beneath Marshall's glare. A cackle escaped Dante.

"He's not wrong. I probably will off myself one of these days."

Two sets of pissed off eyes swung his way. "Go to sleep," they chanted simultaneously.

A wave of exhaustion hit, and his feverish humor vanished. "I think I'm going to be sick."

Dante was back on his feet and leaned over the toilet before he knew what happened. He had never seen two men move so fast. Wulf killed people for a living. It was odd to see him looking concerned about anything, but there was no denying the way his whiskey-colored gaze stayed locked on Dante, waiting to see if he lived. Dante felt like every drop of liquid he had consumed in the last week left his body. He clung to the toilet.

"Are you two enjoying the show?" Dante honestly felt like crying. He hadn't been sick in years, and he wasn't used to being weak, especially in front of a member of his team.

Marshall settled onto the bathroom floor and rubbed his back. "I'm not leaving you to suffer alone." He towed Dante back against his chest and held him as a new round of shaking set in.

Wulf shifted from foot to foot and ran his fingers through his dark hair. "You don't look so good. I'm calling Corey."

Marshall kissed his temple. "Dante doesn't want to risk Rhorey catching this. But if you want to leave Corey's number with me, I'll update him later."

Wulf's gaze moved between them. He looked enraged by Marshall's words, which was fair. Marshall shouldn't know anything about Rhorey. In fact,

Marshall shouldn't know anything about anything. Dante didn't remember telling him anything, but he had been delirious. He might have said anything, yet Marshall was still there, comforting and caring for Dante.

"Fuck this. I'm calling."

Wulf stormed off.

Marshall released a tired-sounding sigh. "Sorry. I tried."

Dante closed his eyes and soaked up the comfort. "It's okay. Thanks for showing up." Dante swallowed. His throat hurt. "I'm sorry for dragging you into my bullshit."

Marshall's hold tightened for a second. "You didn't drag me into anything. I volunteered."

Dante wasn't so sure Marshall would feel the same if Zander sent someone to take him out. For all he knew, there was some channel he needed to go through to vet the people who learned their stories. Dante had never gotten this close to anyone. He shouldn't be held responsible for whatever he said while out of his head. Dante didn't even know how much Marshall knew.

"Do you think you're ready to go back to bed?"

Dante made a helpless gesture. "I really want to brush my teeth and drink something. I feel gross as hell."

"I've got you." Marshall came to his feet, towing Dante to his. He turned on the water in the sink and grabbed Dante's toothbrush. While Dante clung to the counter, Marshall wet his toothbrush and put toothpaste on it. Dante leaned over the sink and Marshall brushed his teeth. He wondered if he should feel stupid or weak, but Marshall took immaculate care of him. Marshall went further for him than anyone ever had. With his teeth brushed, Marshall swept Dante from his feet again and carried him to the bed. "I'll grab you something to drink. Just give me a second."

Dante tried to nod, but he didn't know if he accomplished anything.

Marshall rushed from the room and was back in a flash. "Okay. Let's get some water in you and some fever meds. You're burning up again."

Dante let Marshall do everything for him, short of swallowing. His stomach churned, but he kept the water and pills down. Dante closed his eyes as he settled deeper into his pillows. "Thank you and sorry. I don't even know whose shorts I'm wearing, much less anything I've said the past two days. You probably need to work or whatever."

Marshall sat on the mattress beside him and stroked his hair. "Don't worry about me. I work for myself, so I can work or not work as I need, and you're wearing my shorts," Marshall said with a laugh. It was a nice sound. "I couldn't find any pajamas or anything around here. So when I grabbed an overnight bag to stay with you, I just grabbed some stuff for you too. Why is your apartment so bare? How do you live with next to nothing?"

Dante shrugged. He imagined he looked odd to someone normal, like Marshall. "Most of my stuff is in California. We haven't been working the east coast for long. Plus, I don't really need much." A sigh escaped Dante when Marshall scratched his scalp, easing his grow-ing headache. Everything hurt, includ-ing muscles he hadn't known he possessed, but it felt good beneath Marshall's touch. "Your daughter is lucky." Even Dante heard the way his words came out slurred. "It must be nice to be loved." Sleep weighed heavily on Dante's muscles. He thought Marshall said something, but he was beyond hearing a thing. Darkness swallowed him whole, taking away the pain.

Marshall waited until he knew Dante wouldn't wake before cleaning the bathroom. *Your daughter is lucky. It must be nice to be loved.* Those words wouldn't leave him. Dante kept unwittingly showing pieces of himself, and Marshall didn't like the picture he painted. He was completely unbothered by cleaning messes. That was what he did. Plus, it gave his anger an outlet. Dante talked a lot in his delirious state. Marshall knew way more than he wanted. Dante was supposed to be a good time. He had only stayed when he found Dante sick because he couldn't leave him alone. No one would do that if they were worth a damn. But now, Marshall knew Dante was alone in the world because he had been born into sex trafficking. He didn't own anything or care about anything because he didn't have any long-term goals that included him living much longer. Dante assumed he would live life on the edge until he turned up dead one day. He didn't believe in happy endings. At least, not one where he grew old. Marshall didn't know where to go with all the revelations, so he slept on the couch and waited for Dante to get better.

With the bathroom sanitized, Marshall moved to deal with the angry and visibly jealous twenty-something pacing in the living room. Wulf shot him a bitter glance as he stepped into the room.

Marshall flashed him a smile. He was too tired to deal with youthful rage. "He's sleeping."

Wulf gave a jerky nod. "Corey says all we can do is keep him hydrated and try to control his fever. He can come start an IV, if you want, though."

Marshall moved to the couch and sat. "He drank a bottle of water just now. Dante doesn't want Corey exposed to this, so I'm trying to honor his wishes. If he gets worse, I'll call him. I won't let him get worse for being stubborn."

"It seems like you have everything under control."

Marshall fought an aggravated sigh. He felt every day of his age tonight. "Would you like something to eat or drink? You look tired."

Wulf eyed him. His whiskey-colored eyes held a hint of suspicion, as if people weren't nice to him for no reason. "How do you know Dante?"

"It's complicated."

"I've got time."

Marshall pinched the spot between his eyes where a pain bloomed. His watch dinged, reminding him to breathe. Marshall checked the time. It was one in the morning. "No offense, but if you don't need anything, I've been cat-napping for two days now, trying to grab whatever sleep I can while caring for Dante, and I'm tired."

For a moment, Wulf didn't budge. He held Marshall's stare, like he still was trying to decide if he could trust Marshall with Dante's care, which was ridiculous. If Marshall wanted to hurt Dante, he would have by now. Finally, Wulf gave him a sharp nod. "I'll check on him again."

Marshall shrugged. He was too fucking tired to keep up this cock fight. Wulf let himself out without looking back. Marshall moved to lock the door. He heard Wulf's voice come from the other side.

"Hey, it's Wulf. I need you to look into somebody. Marshall Waverly. He's staying with Dante, and I don't trust the guy."

Marshall's gaze moved to the table where he had left his wallet. It was open. He pinched the spot between his eyes again. No good deed ever went unpunished. At least, not for him. He kept hoping things might change, but nothing ever did. As he moved to make sure nothing was missing from his wallet, he had the same thought that grew bigger every day. Maybe he should leave this town. He could open a new location somewhere else. He could move to California and be closer to Terry. There were other places with pools that needed year-round attention. He could just start somewhere fresh. One of these days, he would do it. Marshall would just disappear.

Chapter Four

LIGHT PENETRATED DANTE'S CLOSED lids. When he opened his eyes, for the first time in days, he thought he might live. His body protested as he rolled from the bed. Every muscle made itself known, and walking to the bathroom felt like a trip through quicksand. After he showered, Dante didn't feel a whole hell of a lot better. He nearly screamed when he gargled with mouthwash after brushing his teeth. His poor throat felt like he had blown an entire football team and they had taken no mercy. After pulling on a pair of clean underwear, he stared at his bed. He swore he could see the germs crawling all over it. His body hated him for being upright for too long, and he swayed. Dante headed for the closet and dragged a clean, fluffy comforter from inside and headed for the living room. He found Marshall sprawled on the couch, wearing nothing but workout shorts.

The poor guy didn't have a blanket or a pillow. Dante felt like shit. Marshall had stayed the whole time Dante had been sick without a single comfort and Dante had felt too bad to argue. Hell, he would have let Marshall sleep with him. The bed was big enough for them both. Marshall probably hadn't wanted to spend quite that much time with Dante's germs. Too bad, though. He slept in the only place Dante wanted to be at the moment, so Dante jammed one knee between Marshall and the couch and climbed on top of the guy. Dante draped himself across Marshall's body like a blanket, letting Marshall's cool skin chill him before covering them with the blanket.

Marshall's arms encircled him. "How are you feeling?"

"Wretched." Dante winced at the sound of his own voice. He was an unpleasant mixture of laryngitis and swallowing nails.

Marshall rubbed his back and made a humming sound that felt good as it vibrated against the ear Dante had pressed to his chest. "At least it feels like your fever has broken."

Dante shrugged and snagged the remote. He found the recording of his favorite cartoon and hit play. It was his comfort show, and he didn't feel like doing anything else. He kissed Marshall's chest without thinking. Dante wanted to tell Marshall how much he appreciated him, but he had never been good at words.

"If I could get it up in my weakened state, you'd definitely be getting fucked right now."

A soft and sexy chuckle had Dante pressing his ear harder against Marshall's chest to savor the sound. "I'm enjoying this just fine."

Dante watched the colorful images dance on the screen, but they didn't bring him peace. "I get why you want him," Dante said before he could stop himself. "Rhett," Dante clarified, even though he knew it was unnecessary. "He's pretty perfect. At least, he is when it comes to Corey. I never blamed Corey for falling for him either."

SPECIALIST

"I'm honestly not sure why you're so convinced I have some insane longing to be with Rhett. I don't. Yes, I asked him out once. Then I met his husband and son and I moved on... to you, I might add."

Dante bit his bottom lip to squelch a smile as he listened to Marshall's heartbeat. He wasn't the jealous type, but Rhett had won the only person Dante had truly wanted for himself. Now Marshall gave him even more affection than Corey had ever shown him, and it messed with Dante's head. Apparently, he had daddy issues. Dante didn't lose sleep over the kink. It didn't take a genius to psychoanalyze him. There was no sense in worrying over things he couldn't change about himself. In fact, Dante enjoyed leaning into the fantasy sometimes. He loved bringing men twice his age to their knees. It was different with Marshall. Dante wanted to do more than seduce Marshall. He thought he might want to keep him, but he was also scared to dream. Life just never worked out for him that way. No one wanted to keep Dante.

"It's been years since I saw this cartoon. I didn't know it still came on. It was my favorite when I was a kid."

Dante nodded, causing his cheek to move up and down, squishing against Marshall's chest. "It's had several spin-offs over the years. Didn't your daughter watch cartoons as a kid?"

Marshall never stopped stroking Dante's back. He was in heaven. "She liked all the shows that came on the public access channel and anything with a princess in it. Otherwise, she didn't watch a lot of TV."

Dante closed his eyes and drifted as he listened to the sound of Marshall's voice. He felt something he never had before, but he couldn't put a name to it. Dante didn't want to move. He felt safe and warm, like he floated on a cloud far away from anything he knew. The moment was exactly what he needed on the heels of being sick. He could stay like this forever. Maybe he would.

Marshall was burning up and had to pee, but he still didn't want to move. A week of sleeping on a couch way too short for him with no covers or pillow had every inch of his body screaming. His back hurt. He swore he had woken up every five minutes for various reasons. His check engine light was on, and Marshall didn't think he would recover any-time soon. Yet he was oddly at peace. Dante's breath fanned across his chest, and he fit in Marshall's arms. He didn't feel the need to do something to busy his mind. He really had to piss, though. That wasn't waiting any longer.

"Sorry, sexy, but my bladder is scream-ing."

With a tired-sounding chuckle, Dante rolled to the side and set Marshall free. Marshall grabbed his overnight bag in the rush to the bathroom. He nearly sighed aloud as he emptied his blad-der. Then he moved to the sink to wash his hands and brush his teeth. His head spun as he stared at himself in the mir-ror. Marshall's dark, thick curls were a mess. He had naturally curly hair, and it didn't like to be tamed. It stood in every direction. There were dark circles under his amber eyes. Marshall winced at the sight. He had done his best to take care of himself over the years, getting Botox and whitening his teeth while moisturizing like a motherfucker. The room spun again, and Marshall gripped the edge of the sink.

He was too old for Dante. Marshall had known that since he looked at Dante's license. He had stayed because Dante needed someone to take care of him. Marshall didn't have that same luxury in his life. He had always been the caretaker, but no one did the same for him. Just like now, Marshall felt the flu setting in. He knew he was getting sick. The weakness in his muscles and the way the room refused to steady said it all, but Marshall didn't have anyone. That was why he couldn't stay. Dante was young, and he needed to be with someone who could keep up, and Marshall needed someone who wanted a partner in life.

He had spent years being nothing more than a parent. Marshall wanted something different now.

With his mind made up, Marshall quickly dressed while praying he could make it home before the worst of the virus hit. After shoving his soiled clothes in his bag, he headed back to the living room. Dante glanced his way. Marshall's heart sighed. Fuck, even still weak from the flu, Dante was sexy as hell. He was sleep-mussed and half dressed. Marshall felt like hell, and he still wanted to take Dante to bed.

"You're dressed."

Marshall winced at the sound of Dante's voice. He wished Dante would stop trying to talk. It sounded like it tore at his vocal cords every time he spoke. "Yeah. Sorry. I've put off a lot of work this week and I've barely been home. I should get going."

Dante moved his feet, making room for Marshall so he could sit down to put on his shoes. He went back to staring at the TV. He didn't meet Marshall's gaze again. "That's cool. I'm sorry if I hurt your business. You didn't have to stay with me."

Even though there was zero emotion in Dante's voice, Marshall swore he felt the way Dante withdrew from him in hurt. Marshall rubbed Dante's leg. "Don't apologize. There's nowhere else I would've rather have been this past week."

Dante snorted, but his smile was real. "Yes, cleaning up puke and listening to feverish rambling is the height of fun."

Marshall shook his head and leaned over to pull on his shoes. That—apparently—was the wrong combination at that exact moment. The world tilted and went black. Then there was nothing.

Chapter Five

EVEN THOUGH DANTE STILL didn't have an ass-ton of energy, he drove to Marshall's work. For now, Marshall slept peacefully, and Dante needed to get back before he woke up and freaked, especially since Dante had left him in Wulf's care. Wulf wasn't happy. To be fair, Wulf was never happy, but he owed Dante a favor. Marshall had said he had fallen behind on work. Dante couldn't let that pass. He was behind because of Dante. Since he was sick, he wouldn't be catching up anytime soon. That was on Dante. He had to make it right.

The office building Marshall owned was actually a house in a subdivision that had been converted into a business. It had a pool out back. Dante didn't know if that was for training purposes or if Marshall was just a fun boss. Probably both, if Dante had to guess. The front door to the office was open. Only a glass screen door kept in the air. Dante walked in like he had every right to be there. That was how he did everything, bold as hell.

A red-haired girl who looked close to thirty glanced up from her desk as he came through the door. Her bright red lipstick complemented her pale face. It was obvious she was someone who stayed put together. "Hi. How can I help you?"

Dante shifted his sunglasses from his face to the top of his head. "Hey. I wasn't sure who I should talk to about Marshall, but he has the flu. He says he's behind on some work, so I needed to sort that out."

A line appeared between her eyebrows. She glanced behind her at an open office. "Um. Beau is the manager here. I suppose he could help."

"Thanks."

He stepped around her desk.

She didn't stop him.

Dante poked his head into the office. A brown-haired guy with a dark tan sat at a messy desk, drinking coffee. He paused with his cup lifted to his lips as Dante stepped inside his office. "Hey, Beau, right?" He paused as he realized he hadn't asked the woman her name. Dante glanced behind him. "What's your name?"

She smiled. "Daisy."

He nodded and turned back to Beau. "Daisy says you're the man to see about taking over for Marshall while he's sick."

Beau's eyebrows rose. His hazel eyes looked nice—like he was a good person. Dante couldn't explain that reasoning. He was just good at reading people. "Marshall is sick? Damn. I told him he wasn't looking too good the last time I saw him."

Dante nodded. "It's my fault. He caught it from me."

Beau set his coffee aside. He didn't look as friendly any longer. "Who are you again?"

A smile that felt wicked tugged at Dante's lips. "I never said, but I'm Dante."

Beau flashed him a tight smile. "Sorry. He's never mentioned your name. Are you dating Terry?"

"Nope." It took all of Dante's control not to start shit at Marshall's work. It was obvious Beau was trying to see if he should be jealous. This was definitely a man who had fucked Marshall and hoped to do it again. Dante needed to get moving. "Anyhow, that's all I needed. He isn't in good enough shape to deal with anything right now, and I didn't want the place falling apart in his absence."

Beau's smile turned feral. "Yeah. I think I've got it. I've been managing this place since before you were born."

Dante's eyebrows snapped together. He didn't like Beau's tone. Dante was trying to help Marshall. Not swing dicks with some dude who was obviously too stupid to have tied Marshall down before Dante had come along. "Yikes. Why did that dig sound like it came from a place of jealousy?"

"Do I have a reason to be jealous?" Beau hadn't played dumb, and Dante appreciated that. That's why he was honest.

"If you think you have any shot of taking Marshall from me, then yes. You should definitely feel some way about things."

The muscle in Beau's jaw ticked, but he kept his cool otherwise. "You can let Marshall know things are good here. But please ask him to call me when he can." Beau paused and held Dante's stare. "Otherwise, I have to wonder if you're who you say you are or if I need to come looking for him."

A smile snapped to Dante's lips. "Oh. He has fire, after all." Dante didn't bother agreeing to tell Marshall anything. He would, but it was too much fun, leaving Beau guessing. Dante laughed as he headed for the door. Poor Marshall. He really needed someone who genuinely wanted him. Dante did.

With Marshall's work covered, Dante headed for Corey's. He didn't think he was contagious any longer, and he needed meds for Marshall. Corey had a full-on pharmacy at his place. Dante could dart in, grab a script, and get home before Marshall missed him. It was his turn to play nursemaid. Even though he was still recovering, he wouldn't let Marshall down. At Corey's, he typed the code in at the gate and circled around the property so he could enter through the medical area. All the members of the team had access cards.

He hoped he could sneak in, grab meds, and get out without too much chitchat. He was ready to get back to Marshall. Unfortunately, as he came through the back door, he ran into Corey immediately.

Corey looked up from organizing his medical files. "Hey. You're alive."

Dante's smile was genuine. There was a part of Dante that would always be in love with Corey. It had always been a hopeless love, but Dante was fucked up like that. Lots of people had wanted him for sex over the years. When people showed him genuine affection, he got in his feelings.

"Yeah. It feels like it was a near miss."

Corey pulled a face. "I'll bet."

Corey's blue eyes always got under his skin, but it wasn't as bad today. "So, hey," he said, getting down to business. "My friend got sick, taking care of me. Can I get some of those pills for him? The ones you prescribed for me."

Without missing a beat, Corey grabbed his keys and unlocked the medicine room. "Sure. Is it Wulf? I know he was worried about you."

Dante rubbed the back of his neck. "No. It's Marshall."

Corey stared at him in silence, blinking. "As in the Marshall who got Rhett fired from his job," Corey said after a moment. "That Marshall?"

Dante rolled his eyes. "He didn't get Rhett fired from his job."

Corey turned away and grabbed a box of the pills Marshall needed. "So he says, but he's the only person who knew

Rhett had that porn channel and also knew Rhett was a teacher."

Dante accepted the pills. "Thanks." He didn't leave. Instead, he shifted from foot to foot and debated with himself. He spoke before he could talk himself out of it. "I'm the one who sent the anonymous tip to Rhett's school." Dante wasn't proud of himself, but neither was he ashamed. Rhett had run a subscription-only porn channel while teaching at the high school. He had gotten fired when the school received a tip about the channel. Since Marshall had been a subscriber and his daughter had been in Rhett's class, Marshall looked like the obvious candidate for the whistleblower. Dante couldn't let Marshall take the blame.

Corey spent another full thirty seconds staring at Dante before finding his voice. "Why?"

He didn't sound hurt or angry. That gave Dante strength. "Rhorey needed him here."

And Dante didn't regret a damn thing. Corey would never love Dante, but Dante could make sure he got the life he deserved. Rhett loved Corey and Rhorey. He was sunshine and bubbles and everything Dante wished he had for a parent. Corey and Rhorey had a chance with Rhett that Dante would never get. So he had cleared an obstacle for the couple. Rhett was needed here, and Corey could afford to support them. Someone had to make it happen.

Corey's chest expanded on a deep breath. "Well. Huh."

It was obvious Corey was at a loss for words. While Dante didn't feel an ounce of guilt for anything, he didn't think he could handle seeing Corey mad at him.

"I'll go. Thanks again." Dante turned to leave with a lump in his throat. His eyes burned. He wasn't an emotional person, but Corey meant something to him no one else did.

"Dante."

Dante stopped, but he didn't turn around. Unfortunately, Corey refused to say anything else until Dante turned. When he did, Corey pulled the door closed to his medicine supply closet and headed Dante's way. Dante stood still, unsure of what would happen next. He startled when Corey unexpectedly hugged him.

Dante held tightly to the box of pills and didn't know what to do with his arms.

Corey squeezed him harder. "It's okay. I know you were looking out for me. I'm not mad."

A shuddered breath escaped Dante. Until that moment, he hadn't realized how much it mattered if he hurt Corey.

Corey took a step back but held on to Dante's shoulders so he couldn't get away. "Next time, let's talk before you act on that big of an impulse, okay? Tell Marshall I hope he feels better soon and call me if he needs anything."

Dante nodded. He couldn't look away from Corey. Dante realized something monumental. He didn't love Corey in a romantic way. Corey was more like a hero to him. His approval meant more than anyone else's did. Now he wanted to go home to Marshall. That was where he belonged.

"You have to take these pills Corey gave me."

A groan rose in Marshall's throat. Everything hurt, and he was dying.

"God, I really hope I wasn't this bad of a patient. Open your eyes, Marsh. You have to drink something and take meds now. Don't make me get Wulf in here to help me."

Another groan escaped Marshall as he fought harder to move. "No. He hates me. I overheard him asking someone to investigate me."

"Okay. I definitely need to look into that because that wasn't cool, but you still have to take these meds."

Marshall forced himself into a sitting position and then collapsed, fighting for each breath against the headboard. The room tilted. "Shit. I haven't felt this bad in years." He focused on Dante. His eyeliner was back, making his gorgeous light green eyes pop. "Fuck. You're beautiful."

A bright smile lit Dante's face. "Come on, gorgeous. Take these pills."

Marshall's throat burned as he washed a handful of whatever Dante gave him down with ice cold water. He winced. Everything still hurt, but he was grateful for Dante. "Thank you. Without you, I guess I would've gone home and died. No one else would take care of me like this."

Dante waved off his thanks. "Nah. That's not true. Beau would've gladly taken my place."

"How do you know Beau?" His brain felt slow.

Without meeting his stare, Dante picked up a forehead thermometer and took Marshall's temperature. He sucked in a hiss. "One hundred and three point nine. I'll be right back." Dante rushed into the bathroom and came back with a wet washcloth. "Let's put this on your forehead."

Marshall settled back into the pillows.

Dante placed the cold cloth on Marshall's forehead as he answered. "I went by your work to let them know you're sick and won't be in for a while."

"That was nice of you. Really nice." Even Marshall heard how weak his voice sounded, but his lips just kept moving. "Trust me when I say Beau most definitely would not have taken care of me. No one does. My whole life, I've been the one who takes care of everyone else.

You get used to it, but then again, you don't."

"Trust me. I understand, but what about when you were a kid? You have parents, right?"

Marshall shook his head. It hurt. He ground his back teeth for a moment to stave off the pounding before responding. "My dad left my mom right after she brought my little brother home from the hospital. I was four, but still I knew it would fall to me. Everything falls to me." Marshall took a breath and savored the way Dante stroked his chest and stomach, soothing him. He couldn't stop spilling his entire life story. "I don't remember how old I was when I started doing everything while my mom stayed gone. She went to school full-time and worked full-time. I cooked, cleaned, and raised my brother like I was the parent. Then I started cleaning pools for extra money at sixteen, got my girlfriend pregnant when I was twenty-one, and the rest is history. I never stopped working or taking care of people. Now I'm old and I've lost my chance at having anything I wanted for myself." Marshall's throat swelled. He didn't understand why saying those words hurt tonight or why he bothered saying them at all. Being sick really fucked with his head. He was emotional as hell.

"You're not old."

Marshall snorted. That was a mistake. The sound ripped at his throat, making him immediately suck in a gasp. Then shaking struck from nowhere. He locked his back teeth.

Dante climbed into bed with him and hauled him into his arms. "I've got you. I'll keep you warm."

SPECIALIST

With his eyes closed and Dante wrapped around him, sleep tried pulling Marshall under. He fought it for a moment while savoring the attention. Dante could have accepted his help and then left Marshall to suffer, but he hadn't. He was the first person in memory to put Marshall ahead of himself. It was unexpected and kind of nice. Marshall didn't want to get attached. Dante was still half his age and would find someone else who matched him soon enough. Marshall would fade into memory. That was okay. He knew how the world worked. Marshall accepted that fate. He wasn't alone today. That was all that mattered. He would take what he could get.

Chapter Six

GOING BACK TO WORK after two weeks off should have left Marshall refreshed. Instead, he fought the urge to throw in the towel. He didn't want to do anything but go back to Dante's and continue being spoiled. Unfortunately, he no longer had a fever, and they had to get back to real life. As he came through the door at his office, Daisy smiled and waved, but kept up her end of the conversation with a customer on the phone. Marshall nodded and kept moving. He needed to make sure payroll had gone out on time in his absence and double check some billing issues. Beau wasn't in his office, which wasn't out of the ordinary. He preferred being out in the field, working with his hands and passing the time. Marshall sat behind his desk and sipped his coffee before getting to work.

The morning passed while he ran numbers through his head. Random thoughts about Dante kept pulling him off track. He stopped himself five different times from texting Dante. The last thing Marshall wanted was for Dante to get sick of him. Plus, Marshall really needed to put Dante behind him. They had their fun and took care of each other through an illness. In no way did that mean they were in a relationship. He had to remember that. Reality was back. He had to face it.

"Hey, you're back."

Marshall's gaze shot to the door. Beau leaned against the frame, smiling. "Hey. Yeah. Barely. I haven't been sick like that in ages. How have things been around here?"

Beau shrugged and straightened. "You know I've got your back. The ship is still afloat." Before Marshall could correct Beau's assumption that Marshall had thought the place would sink without him, Beau moved on. "Would you like to go to lunch?"

AKA buy him lunch. Marshall already knew his role in the game. He checked his watch. "Wow. Is it lunch time already? Sure. What did you have in mind?"

"I was thinking we could hit that Mexican restaurant in West End."

Marshall wasn't sure he was quite up for food yet, but he still stood. He didn't have to get anything once they were there. "All right, but you're driving."

Beau's hazel eyes danced with laughter. "Fair enough since you're paying."

Marshall shook his head as they headed out. He would likely fall out in shock if Beau ever paid for a damn thing, so Marshall wasn't the least bit surprised to have called it on this one. They didn't speak again until Beau pointed his Navigator toward West End and Marshall couldn't jump from the moving SUV.

"So... Dante."

Marshall kept his gaze locked on the road. "What about him?"

"I just haven't heard his name before. That's all."

"Mhmm." Marshall didn't bother saying anything else since Dante wasn't Beau's business.

"He's a bit... young, isn't he?"

Marshall shot Beau an irritated glance. Not that he noticed since he was busy driving. "I didn't see you taking care of me while I had the flu."

Beau shot him an annoyed look. "What good does it do for us both to get sick?"

Marshall hummed. That was what he thought. "I'm just saying."

Beau's knuckles turned white on the steering wheel. "Does Terry know?"

"Why would Terry know?"

Beau didn't say anything else.

Marshall let it drop. His relationship or nonexistent relationship with Dante had nothing to do with Beau. It was also no one's business but Dante's and his. By the time they were seated at a booth at Beau's favorite restaurant, with chips and salsa in front of them, Marshall considered the topic dead. He had been happier, even while sick, these past few weeks than he had been in years. Marshall didn't care to hear anyone's opinion on the matter.

"See, Dante. I told you. You can't even trust the guy out of your sight for four full hours."

Marshall's chin shot up from the menu as Dante shoved his way into Marshall's side of the booth and Wulf bullied his way into the booth on Beau's side. As his gaze collided with the heavily lined and gorgeous green eyes he had come to adore seeing, a bright smile snapped to Marshall's lips.

"Hey. Where did you come from?"

Dante kissed the tip of his nose. "Home. Wulf texted me you were out with another man, so I had to see for myself." He stole a chip.

A laugh burst from Marshall. "You have Wulf stalking me too?" He didn't bother looking Wulf's way. Marshall already knew the guy hated him.

Dante shrugged as he nibbled on the corner of the chip. "He chose to do so of his own volition, but it seems he wasn't wrong. Here you are... un-alone."

Marshall's smile never dimmed. He shouldn't have been happy about Dante's obvious jealousy, but he was. It had to mean something. He motioned Beau's way. "Dante, meet my little brother, Beau. Beau, Dante," he said, motioning Dante's way.

Dante looked between them. Finally, his gaze landed on Beau. "You're his brother?"

Beau flashed Dante a tight smile. "Guilty."

Dante's gaze moved between them again.

Wulf ate a chip.

"But you were acting all puffed up and jealous when I stopped by the office to tell you Marshall was sick."

Marshall's eyebrows rose at the claim, but he didn't have time to ask a single question before Dante went after Wulf. "And you. I thought you were all about investigating people against their will. You didn't pull that tidbit up while digging into people's lives?"

Beau pulled a face. "You've been investigating my brother? What's your deal? First, you show up and start acting like I'll tank Marshall's company if he takes off a few days, and now your watchdog is following my brother around and accusing him of cheating. What the fuck is wrong with you two?"

"We're bad people," Wulf said, dipping a chip in the salsa, as if he dealt with this level of bullshit every day.

Beau stared at Wulf, looking exasperated. "You're bad people?"

Wulf nodded. "The worst. We're the ones your momma warned you about." He popped a chip into his mouth.

A laugh burst from Marshall. It was out of his control. The whole situation was insane, and he was having the greatest time of his life.

Everyone looked at him with equal parts irritation.

Marshall didn't have eyes for anyone but Dante. He swallowed his laughter and swiped at his eyes as he held Dante's stare. "You're the best part of my day." It was the realest confession of his life. Meeting Dante was the most wonderful thing to happen to him in a long time. Marshall wanted more of the insanity. As much as he could get until Dante got bored, and then a little more. Bring it on.

If Dante possessed an ounce of shame, he might have been embarrassed. He wasn't happy with Wulf, but he didn't regret anything either. Marshall invited everyone to stay for lunch. They kept touching beneath the table. Their fingers linked. Each time they looked each other's way, their gazes lingered. Dante kept biting his bottom lip, fighting the urge to beg for kisses. He didn't know what was wrong with him, but he couldn't get enough.

When the check came, Dante passed two bills to their server before anyone else could. "I've got it and I don't need any change."

Marshall's lips parted in surprise. He quickly rallied. "I asked you to stay for lunch. It's on me to pay."

Dante shook his head. "Who came up with that bullshit? I've got it."

"Marshall can afford it."

At Beau's offhand comment, Dante shot him an irritated look, but he didn't have to say a word. Wulf scoffed. "Dante could buy this restaurant, if he wanted." Wulf turned his head. He met and held Beau's stare. "I could too, as a matter of fact. I just didn't offer to pay because I understand when someone asks you to lunch, then they're offering to pay. Then you pay the next time. Is that something you understand?"

Dante's eyebrows rose. He had never seen Wulf taunt someone this much. Normally, he never talked at all. Something about Beau obviously pissed him off and he couldn't stop pushing him.

"Yeah, okay." Beau snorted, sounding as condescending as possible. "I know money when I see it. That's all I do all day long is collect from the richest people in town. Neither of you fit the bill, but go off if it makes you feel better about yourself."

Wulf picked up his cellphone from where it sat on the table and clicked around.

Dante looked Marshall's way. He didn't care about anything but the man currently rubbing his thigh.

Marshall looked as if he had been waiting for Dante's attention. "What are your plans for the rest of the day?"

"What the fuck?"

At Beau's loudly spoken question, Dante glanced the pair's way. Beau stared at Wulf's phone, looking horrified yet fascinated.

Marshall squeezed his thigh, pulling Dante's focus back his way. He didn't look as if he cared about anything happening across the table. Dante didn't leave him hanging. "Nothing. I called my boss this morning, and he wants me to take another week to rest before taking any more jobs."

The way Marshall's gaze kept dropping to Dante's mouth told Dante exactly what Marshall wanted. "Beau drove. Otherwise, I'd steal you away while they're focused on bickering."

Dante's gaze moved to Marshall's full lips. He wanted to taste them. Dante licked his lips. "You know, you should really take another week too. It's not good to be out working in this heat while still recovering. I drove. You could come home with me, and I'll bring you back to work whenever you're ready to go back."

Marshall glanced Beau and Wulf's way. They stared at Marshall and Dante, as if disgusted by them. His gaze moved back to Dante. "Let's go."

Beau released a loud, irritated-sounding sigh, but didn't stop them. He looked Wulf's way. "I suppose you need a fucking ride now."

"Don't bother," Wulf snapped behind them as they left the pair behind.

Dante couldn't stop smiling. He would soon have Marshall to himself again.

That was all that mattered to him. As they reached Dante's car, Marshall molded against his back. Dante's eyes closed as he savored being held. For a moment, he couldn't move. Something grew in his chest before swelling in his throat. He wanted so much out of life he had never had. Marshall made him feel like he had a shot at... something. A normal life, maybe. Happiness. When he couldn't stand there any longer without getting weird looks, Dante opened the passenger side door for Marshall.

A sexy soft chuckle rumbled from Marshall. "You know I can open a door, right?"

Dante met Marshall's stare. Marshall's smile slipped away. Dante knew Marshall saw the real version of him at that moment. "I know. There's nothing you can't do for yourself, but you shouldn't have to do everything. Let me take some part of you for myself." All Dante could do was hope Marshall understood what he meant, since he knew he didn't make sense.

For a moment, they simply held each other's stare. Then Marshall's gaze moved over Dante's face, as if searching for an answer for a question only he knew. Finally, Marshall nodded. "All you have to do is tell me what you want, and it's yours."

Dante motioned toward the passenger seat. "Get in so I can take you away. I want to be held."

"I can handle that."

A shiver ran through Dante as he closed the door, shutting Marshall inside. He didn't know where they were headed. Maybe they weren't going anywhere. But today, Marshall belonged to Dante and Dante planned to take as much affection as he could get.

As Dante climbed behind the wheel, Marshall's phone rang. He dug it from his pocket, glanced at the face, and answered.

"Hey, baby girl. How's California life treating you?"

Dante backed from his parking spot and drove, trying to pretend he wasn't eavesdropping.

"Did he now?" Marshall paused for half a second. "First off, that wasn't his business to tell, and second, he's not the same age as you. He's three years older than you."

Ah. It was his daughter. Dante listened closer. He didn't care what Terry thought about them, but Marshall likely did. He recognized this might be a breaking point for them.

Marshall leaned Dante's way and stroked his thigh. "I don't know. We'll have to see." Marshall huffed at whatever Terry said. "Because I just don't know yet. That's why we haven't talked about this. Listen, you're grown now and living on the other side of the country. I need you to understand that I'm allowed to have a life too."

Damn. It didn't sound like things were going well. A wave of nausea washed over Dante. He had hoped for a nice day with Marshall.

"Of course," Marshall said after a moment of listening to Terry. "I'll let you know. I love you. Good luck with your interview. Call me when you land the job."

Dante's gut clenched with desire. Marshall was the dad he wished he would have had. He fought the urge to say how nice it must be to have a parent's support. Dante clenched his back teeth, fighting the jealousy. Terry not only had an amazing dad, but he was also so wonderful, she could call him to bitch about his social life without repercussions. He wondered if she knew how good she had it.

Marshall disconnected the call and laughed. "Beau didn't waste time tattling on me."

Dante didn't want to ask, but he couldn't stop himself. "What did she say?"

Thankfully, Marshall didn't refuse to answer. "At first, she was upset about the age difference. Then she immediately switched to demanding to meet you. I told her we'd have to see."

Dante stared hard at the road and tried to stay calm. "Why just 'we'll see'?"

Marshall didn't answer right away, forcing Dante to look his way. He found Marshall staring at him with his heart in his eyes. Dante swallowed and looked away. Marshall stroked Dante's arm with the back of his hand as he finally answered. "Because you are only three years older than my daughter, and that makes me wonder how long you'll stick around."

Honestly, that was fair. The first few times Dante had touched Marshall, he hadn't intended for it to mean anything at all. He was just another guy. Dante had only been filling a void inside himself. Then Marshall had shown up when no one else would have, and he had stayed. He kept actively working for Dante's affection, and it was addictive. Unfortunately, now that Marshall had voiced his fears, Dante wondered if he didn't give as much to Marshall.

"Am I doing something to make you think I'm going somewhere?"

"No."

At Marshall's immediate answer, Dante tossed him a confused looked. "Then you've lost me. Why do you think I won't stick around?"

Marshall laughed. "I don't know. Maybe because we haven't talked about it, and I didn't want to assume anything. Do you plan to stick around?"

Again, that was fair. Dante wasn't one to talk about shit, but he also shouldn't assume Marshall could read his mind. Dante cleared his throat. He suddenly felt uncomfortable as fuck. There was a real chance he would say the words and Marshall would run for the hills.

After all, Marshall had been single for years. There was no reason for Dante to believe he would change his life just for Dante. Fuck it, though. He was no weak bitch. "I think the real question is, do you plan on sticking around? After all, you're nearly nineteen years older than me and you haven't let anyone lock you down yet. I'd ask if you plan to make me just another notch in your bedpost, but," he flashed Marshall a wicked smile, "I plan to fuck you so good, you can't walk, much less run. Sorry, not sorry, but you're stuck with me."

Marshall set his hand on Dante's thigh, as if settling in for the ride. "Okay. Then I guess I'll let Terry know you'll be meeting, eventually."

Dante felt the satisfaction in his smile, but he couldn't reel it in. Marshall belonged to him. There was no going back for either of them. Now he had to keep his word about fucking Marshall into uselessness. That was only fair.

The day had been absolutely nuts. One second, Marshall had been dragging himself back to work. The next minute, Dante had shown up, obviously ready to show out, thinking Marshall was cheating. The craziest part of all of that was the idea Marshall could cheat on a relationship he hadn't known he was in, but he knew now. Dante wouldn't share. Marshall was good with that, especially since his dick was in Dante's mouth again and Marshall had never been this spoiled.

Marshall was on fire and half crazed. Dante's lubed fingers sawed in and out of Marshall's ass, but Dante purposely didn't let Marshall come. Sweat covered his entire body. Madness scratched at his brain. Marshall snapped.

An evil-sounding laugh burst from Dante as Marshall shoved Dante on to his back. His laughter turned to moans as Marshall crouched over his dick and impaled himself. With his head thrown back and sucking air, Marshall bounced on Dante's cock, taking what he wanted. Dante made sounds that drove Marshall wild. He also stroked Marshall's erection, helping Marshall along. Everything went silent and then exploded into colorful, beautiful sound. Marshall gasped for air while his cum coated Dante's torso. He couldn't stop staring at the blond beauty beneath him. Dante open-mouth fought for air as he came.

"Goddamn. Yes. Fuck, Marsh. You feel so good. I want you all the time."

Marshall fell forward and claimed Dante's lips. They struggled to catch their breath while their tongues played. Marshall felt good on the inside—like he never had before. He couldn't come down from the high. Their entire day had been like this. Dante's bedroom was pitch dark, except for the light spilling from the bathroom and casting a glow over them. Marshall had no clue what time it was. They had been wrapped up in each other all day. Exhaustion quickly set in, making his muscles weak. He rolled to the side and set Dante free of his weight. Their kisses turned sweet.

Dante groaned as he finally pulled away and rolled from the bed. "Fuck. I don't want to move, but I can't let you fall asleep with cum all over you."

Personally, Marshall didn't care, but whatever. He floated on a cloud of euphoria as he watched Dante head inside the bathroom nude. His lanky body was sexy as fuck. Despite his weakened state, giddiness still ran through Marshall. He still couldn't believe they were a couple now. It felt too good to be true. Marshall hadn't known how much he wanted this until he had it.

Dante returned with a wet washcloth. Marshall's stomach clenched with a desire that never ebbed at the sight of Dante's semi-hard cock. He didn't understand how he could still want Dante after a day of nonstop playing, but he did. His heavy eyelids didn't care about his heart's desire. After cleaning Marshall, Dante leaned in and swiped his lips across Marshall's.

"Get some sleep, sexy. You'll need—" A buzzing sound cut off Dante's claim.

Dante snagged his phone from the nightstand. "I'm sorry, gorgeous. I have to go to work. You sleep, though."

"I thought they told you to take another week?"

Dante shrugged. "If it's a big job, then it's like that sometimes."

Marshall wanted to whine about missing cuddles, but he already knew he would be asleep in ten seconds whether Dante joined him or not. "It's okay. Be careful."

Dante leaned over and brushed noses with him before stealing another kiss.

Marshall kept his eyes closed as Dante moved away. Part of him drifted, but a whooshing sound had his heavy eyelids slightly lifting. He still felt more asleep than awake as he watched Dante slide away part of the wall, revealing a hidden room. Marshall drifted in and out, catching only moments of Dante pulling on a hazmat suit before tying the top half around his waist. Next, Dante pulled on a gun shoulder holster before holstering two guns. Sleep carried Marshall away before his mind registered a thing. He was too tired to care. It never occurred to him something might be amiss. He just needed sleep. Everything felt like a dream.

Chapter Seven

MARSHALL: *I FOUND A rose on the pillow beside me this morning. Who could've done such a thing?*

Dante: *There are eleven more at my place, waiting for you to get here.*

Marshall: *I'll see you soon.*

SPECIALIST

Dante: *Did you really cook me breakfast before you left?*

Marshall: *Of course. I knew you'd be tired from working all night when you got home. I also knew you'd skip breakfast if it wasn't waiting for you. Eat before going to sleep.*

Dante: *Yes, Daddy.*

Marshall: *Good boy.*

Dante: *That's my line.*

Marshall: *You can't play both roles.*

Dante: *Watch me.*

Dante: *I might have broken into your house. Maybe you should come home and see your surprise.*

Marshall: *You're always spoiling me. I never get the chance to reciprocate. I've gained ten pounds since we started dating from your surprises.*

Dante: *So? Me too. Happiness looks good on us. But if I promise it's not food, will you come home now?*

Marshall: *You don't have to promise anything. I'm always willing to rush to wherever you are.*

Dante: *Hurry.*

While gathering his things to leave, Marshall couldn't stop smiling. Truthfully, he never stopped grinning like an idiot for long since he started dating Dante four months ago. He felt like he walked on clouds. When he had moved Terry to California at the beginning of the summer, so she would have plenty of time to find a job and get settled before starting Cal State, he had fully expected to use his newfound freedom to play the field. There was no way he could have seen Dante coming. Marshall headed for the door and walked straight into Beau.

A smile lit Beau's face. "Hey. Where're you headed?"

Marshall realized he should feel guilty for leaving early… again, but he didn't. "I'm dipping out for the day."

Beau's smile faltered, but he visibly fought to keep it in place. "We might have to revisit my salary if you keep leaving me to handle everything."

It took everything Marshall possessed not to roll his eyes. "You make three times what anyone else in your position makes. I think you'll be fine if you have to do what I actually hired you to do, which is take my place so I don't have to work," Marshall reminded him, in case Beau forgot that was why he made so much in the first place. It had always been Marshall's intention to position himself where he wouldn't have to work at all anymore.

"I know you hired me to take your place here. It's just that I'm used to having you around. It seems like I don't see you that much anymore."

Now Marshall felt guilty. "I know. For once, I'm getting to enjoy life and..." Marshall shrugged.

Beau nodded. "I get it. You don't have to explain. Have a good day."

Marshall's guilt doubled. "Maybe we can get lunch tomorrow."

"Okay." Beau brightened.

A weight lifted from Marshall's chest. "Think about where we're going today, and I'll see you about this time tomorrow."

With a nod, Beau moved along to his office. Marshall nearly sighed in relief before darting out the door. He knew he was tied up in Dante right now and most people didn't understand, but everyone else had a life outside of him. For all of Beau's acting hurt, he lived like a single guy, partying and enjoying the money Marshall paid him. While Marshall had been focused on raising his daughter, he had never once begrudged everyone else moving on with their lives. He wished everyone could be the same for him for once.

By the time Marshall got home, he—once again—no longer cared if anyone was onboard. He parked in the garage and cut through the kitchen, expecting anything. He needed to give Dante a key so the guy could stop breaking in every time he wanted to see Marshall. Dante had proven Marshall's security system was useless. Even though Dante's car was also parked in the garage, which was a whole other wonderment to Marshall, Dante was nowhere to be seen. Marshall trailed from room to room, searching. He backtracked to the bedroom and noticed the light was on in his bathroom. Marshall headed inside. He found Dante waiting in a bubble bath with two glasses of champagne.

A smile exploded across Marshall's face at the sight. "I see my surprise is already unwrapped."

Dante's grin was unrepentant as hell. "I've been keeping the water warm. Get in."

While holding Dante's stare, Marshall removed everything from his pockets and took off his shirt. Dante bit his bottom lip and dragged his gaze down Marshall's body. It was empowering as hell, being with Dante. Despite the difference in their ages, Dante always made Marshall feel irresistible. The second he was nude, Marshall crossed the room and climbed into the tub. He sat facing Dante.

Dante handed him a glass of champagne. "We're celebrating."

Marshall hesitated as his fingers wrapped around the glass. He prayed he hadn't forgotten something important. It was Halloween, but surely Dante didn't celebrate Halloween. "We are?"

Dante nodded. "It's my birthday."

"Fuck." Marshall's heart dropped. "I didn't know." But he did and he had forgotten. He had looked at Dante's license and used his birthdate to pick up Dante's prescription back when he had the flu. But that had been four months ago, and Marshall had been too engrossed in their day-to-day life to even think about it.

Dante's smile didn't falter. He shrugged and took a sip of his drink of champagne before responding. "There's no rule that says I can't throw my own party for two."

Marshall set the glass aside. "There are unwritten rules. You should've said something. I would've gone above and beyond. Fuck." He was irrationally angry with himself. "I want to go all out for you. Stupidly, I've been thinking about what I wanted to do for you for Christmas and your birthday just fucking got lost. I'm so, *so* sorry."

Dante set his glass aside and shifted to his knees. He kept moving until he straddled Marshall's lap. "Stop. This is what I want. Just you and me. A tub full of bubbles."

Marshall's head fell back against the edge of the tub. It didn't matter what Dante said. He wanted to do more. He couldn't hide his disappointment. Marshall had let himself down. "I'm buying you a gift."

Dante smirked and scooted closer, ensuring the friction between them couldn't go unnoticed. "What do you want to give me?"

The world. That thought hit Marshall so hard and fast, he lost his breath. His arms encircled Dante and held on tight. Everything was always ridiculously easy between them. The truth shouldn't have surprised Marshall, but it did. "My heart."

Dante's smile grew. "That's already mine. You said you wanted to buy me something."

Marshall couldn't bring himself to smile. The moment felt too important. "Tell me you're in love with me too, and I'll give you absolutely anything you want. Just name it."

Dante's smile slowly slipped away as heat filled his features. He moved until his lips hovered an inch from Marshall's. Marshall's eyes automatically fell closed, anticipating Dante's kiss. "I love you too."

Marshall closed the final inch between them so fast, their teeth bumped. He had to know how those words tasted. Their tongues clashed. He swore Dante's hands were everywhere. Marshall forgot everything. One second, all Marshall could think about was how in love he was with life. The next, his entire body was on fire. Lust gnawed at his skin. Dante owned Marshall's mouth while he stroked their cocks. All Marshall could do was hold on for the ride. The way he always did with Dante. Dante was one hundred percent in charge of this relationship. It felt fucking amazing. Marshall had let go of being the driver of his life four months ago, and Dante never let him down. He had never felt happier or freer. Sometimes he thought he could taste Dante's cockiness. He loved it.

Dante torc his mouth away. "That's it, sexy. Come for me. I'm about to wring you out tonight."

Marshall strained against Dante's palm.

Dante threw his head back. A sexy roar tore from his throat. At the sound, Marshall blew. He swore he saw stars. The air left his lungs. Then Dante was back, tongue stroking tongue. Marshall's muscles slowly relaxed. His soul hummed. He wished they could stay there forever. Marshall had found everything he ever wanted. It was in his arms.

Birthdays never really meant much to Dante. It wasn't like anyone had ever celebrated his. Once Marshall learned it was Dante's day, he did his best to make it perfect. The moment they stepped out of the tub, Marshall had grabbed his phone and clicked around. In less than an hour, dinner, cake, flowers, and balloons had arrived. Two hours later, a final gift had shown up on the doorstep. Marshall had held Dante's stare while he helped Dante put on the gold necklace. Dante hadn't gotten a chance to inspect the small charm attached. Their lips had met, and the night had been lost. Dante had gotten inside Marshall as quickly as possible and stayed as long as he possibly could. By the time darkness filled the room, Dante had fulfilled his promise. On his stomach, Marshall was a heap of useless muscles and Dante's cum leaked from his ass. Dante wanted to pat himself on the back, but he was too tired. When his phone buzzed on the nightstand, he thought he might cry.

"No." The word dragged on as Dante rolled over and snagged the device. As always, it was only an address. He had to go to work. "Goddamn."

Marshall lifted his head. "It's your birthday. Can you skip it?"

He wished. "Unfortunately, no. Expansion to this coast is still fairly new. It's only me and two other guys. Most jobs take all three of us."

Marshall held his stare, as if he saw too much. In fact, sometimes, Dante felt like Marshall knew everything. It was only a matter of time—if they stayed together—Dante would have to tell Marshall everything. That was a tricky move, though. If Marshall accepted him, then that was the best-case scenario. If they broke up, Zander would likely have Marshall killed. That was why Dante hadn't made any late-night confessions. Marshall was safe as long as he knew nothing. Of course, Dante didn't actually have to tell Marshall anything. Technically, he hadn't lied about anything. Dante cleaned up crime scenes. Marshall didn't need to know it was his people committing the crimes.

Impulsively, Dante snagged a rose from the bedside table, from the bouquet Marshall had ordered for him, and dragged the petals down Marshall's spine. He watched chill bumps rise on Marshall's skin. Dante had never been more tempted to stay. He set the rose on the pillow next to Marshall.

"To hold my place until I get back."

Marshall smiled. His eyes crinkled in the corners.

Dante couldn't look away. He never expected to fall in love, but here they were. "I love you. Get some sleep."

Marshall nodded. "I love you too. Be careful."

Dante stood and started gathering his things. "Always." After he dressed, Dante stole a quick kiss and headed for the door. He set the alarm before he left. Dante drove home on autopilot and changed into his bio gear, with thoughts of Marshall clouding his brain. In spirit, Dante never left Marshall's bed even as he arrived at the shipping yard.

Wulf waited for him. "It's the usual shit. A shipment of kids arrived earlier. Ender took three guys out, and the rest scattered, leaving the kids behind. Jericho and Ender are transporting the kids to Dr. A's place."

"Cool. I guess we should get started." They had to scrub the scene and make all traces of tonight disappear. Zander had the local authorities under control, but they couldn't risk anyone coming across the scene. Before he pulled on his helmet, Wulf touched his arm, stopping him. Dante met his stare.

SPECIALIST

"Happy birthday."

A smile exploded across Dante's face. As much as he always pretended not to care about being forgotten, he wanted to have a normal life. Like everyone else, he wanted to have one day where everyone thought of him. "Thanks."

Wulf nodded and turned away.

Dante looked down and inspected the necklace Marshall gave him. It was the first moment he had time to do so. It was a tiny flat and round piece of gold with even smaller writing. Dante brought it close to his face. *My love is always with you.* With a huge smile, Dante finished gearing up and went to work.

Even while surrounded by dead people, Dante went right back to thinking about Marshall. He still hadn't met Terry yet. It wasn't that Marshall didn't want him to meet her. Dante knew that. They just hadn't made the trip to California yet. Dante had been to Cali a few times since they started dating and he had thought about looking Terry up while on the west coast, but he didn't want to be weird. Honestly, though, not meeting Marshall's daughter was the only thing stopping Dante from doing something he wanted more than anything. He wanted to ask Marshall to marry him. Marshall had a birthday in a month a half, right before Christmas. It seemed kind of like a cop out to use the day as an excuse to propose, but that was Dante's plan. Obviously, he would get Marshall a real gift too, but he also wanted Marshall to accept the ring he had already bought and carried with him everywhere. They just fit. Marshall felt like he belonged to Dante. Dante needed to make it permanent. He wanted to be a family. Dante wanted to *have* a family.

SPECIALIST

The blood, puke, and human feces surrounding him didn't faze Dante. He had seen so much in his life, he may as well be a hundred. Maybe that was why the age difference between Marshall and him didn't bother him. Not only did love not care about age, on the inside, Dante was old as fuck. He had lived three lifetimes. Dante had been through it all. Now life with Marshall felt like peace at last. He needed to know it was forever.

Dante moved toward the first body. The overweight and unkempt man was on his side in an unnatural position. Dante didn't even see these men as people. They were monsters wearing human skin. Likely, they had spent the trip across the ocean taking advantage of as many children as they could, breaking them in before they were auctioned. Unfortunately, Dante recalled his trip vividly. That was why he couldn't stop doing his part to make these men disappear. Not even for Marshall. Dante might have kicked the body before rolling it onto his back. He didn't think he could be blamed. Some bitterness never left.

A loud noise startled him, taking his breath. Then the breath didn't return. His brain moved slower than normal, as if time itself stopped. Dante heard his name called, but it sounded far away. Beady dark eyes stared up at him, looking crazed and very much alive before his head exploded. Blood splattered his helmet, blocking him from seeing. He felt himself falling, but he couldn't stop it from happening. The pain hit last, exploding through his chest. But his last thoughts were still of Marshall. He was at home, thinking Dante would return soon. No air would fill Dante's lungs.

SPECIALIST

He recognized the rattle in his throat. Dante would never see Marshall again. This was the end he had always known he would have. How sad.

Chapter Eight

"GET UP. FUCK. YOU have to wake up."

Marshall's eyes shot open as the words penetrated his brain. He was exhausted beyond what could be considered healthy. When his mind cleared, he scrambled into a sitting position, keeping a tight grasp on the blankets.

"What the fuck are you doing in my house?"

Wulf wore the same white hazmat suit Dante wore to work. Blood coated the material. His eyes were wild. "Get the fuck up, Marshall. We have to go now."

Marshall's heart raced and his pulse pounded in his ears. He was too disoriented to make his brain work properly. But Wulf looked younger than usual and panicked in a way that called to Marshall's parental side. "What's wrong?"

Wulf met and held Marshall's stare, and Marshall knew. He scrambled from the bed, uncaring about his nudity.

"Tell me on the way."

Marshall pulled on a pair of workout shorts and a t-shirt he had worn to bed two nights ago and still littered the floor. Somehow, even in his rush, he still remembered his phone, keys, and wallet. Wulf headed for the door and Marshall followed. He stamped into a pair of old tennis shoes without bothering with socks. In his heart, he knew it was Dante's blood on Wulf's clothes. It didn't even matter what happened. Marshall just needed to get to Dante.

An unmarked white panel van waited in the driveway. It was still running. Wulf jumped behind the wheel. Marshall climbed into the passenger seat. They backed from the driveway before Marshall even shut the door. Wulf drove twice the speed limit. He rambled, looking a panicked mess.

"We were told everyone was dead. The guy should've been dead. Hell, I even checked for pulses before Dante got there. No one was moving. It doesn't make sense. I don't understand what happened."

Marshall could barely breathe, much less follow Wulf's words. They hit a dip in the road and Marshall's ass left the seat, making him realize he didn't have on his seatbelt. Wulf made a left-hand turn and Marshall thought maybe two wheels left the ground, but he couldn't think clearly enough to decide. He needed to know about Dante.

"What happened?"

"That mother fucker shot him," Wulf yelled, punching the steering wheel. "I didn't even think to check for weapons. They were dead. It never even occurred to me there might be any danger."

A roaring began in Marshall's ears. His vision blurred. Then they were through a gate and circling a large house. Marshall's mouth moved even as his brain stayed locked in a haze of shock. "Where are we? Aren't we going to the hospital? Please tell me he's not dead."

Wulf didn't respond. He threw the van in park and was out the door before the vehicle stopped rocking.

Marshall followed, with no clue where they were headed. He just needed to get to Dante, and he knew Wulf would lead him there. Wulf scanned a badge at the unmarked door, and it unlocked. Light poured out as they headed inside. Wulf turned left. Marshall followed. It was a hospital of some type. There were dozens of dirty children huddled together while nurses moved between them, checking vitals. Wulf went through a set of swinging doors and there he was.

Marshall practically shoved Wulf aside to get to Dante. He looked like he was sleeping, but the machines connected to him said otherwise. Rhett's husband, Corey, was there. He wore a doctor's coat and looked solemn as hell. Marshall couldn't see anything but Dante.

His will gave out as he reached Dante's side. He couldn't draw a full breath through the panic. Marshall bent and pressed his forehead to Dante's chest while sucking air. Tears pressed at the backs of his eyes, refusing to be held at bay. They had just been together. This couldn't be real. He swore he could still hear Dante saying he loved him and promising to return soon. This had to be a dream. A horrible nightmare.

Someone squeezed his shoulder. "He couldn't be in better hands. Come on. I brought you a chair."

Marshall straightened and swiped at his eyes. He found Rhett waiting. It seemed so weird to him now that he had once been obsessed with the idea of winning Rhett. Now there was no one but Dante.

If Dante was gone, Marshall didn't know how to survive it, but there would never be anyone else again. He accepted the chair Rhett set at the edge of the bed.

Marshall took Dante's hand, hoping he knew he was there before focusing on Rhett and Corey. "Tell me." He already knew it was bad. Nothing kept his cocky boy from him. Marshall wasn't prepared, but he needed to know.

Corey nodded, as if satisfied Marshall could handle it. "He took one bullet to the torso. It bounced around, shattering several ribs before becoming lodged in his lung, collapsing it. He lost a lot of blood, but I was able to remove the bullet. Unfortunately, he lost part of the lung. He's young and strong. If he wakes up, we'll go from there."

If. That one tiny word stood out above the rest, yet Marshall refused to accept that. "Why are you saying if?"

Corey looked like he tried to stay professional, but his eyes said a different story. He cared about Dante. This hurt him too. "He went without enough oxygen for longer than I like and lost too much blood. That's an ugly combination. I just don't know what will happen."

"He'll wake up." Marshall heard the confidence in his voice. He knew Dante. Marshall settled into the chair, prepared to wait as long as it took. If there was breath left in his body, Dante would live too. That was a promise. They were in this together.

Wulf felt half mad. His mind bounced all over the place. This was his fault. It was on him. He had been the first to arrive for cleanup. That made it his duty to ensure everyone was dead who was supposed to be dead, and no one was alive who needed saving. He had failed. Because of that, Dante might never wake up. This was who Wulf was, though. He was that guy who always fucked up. Wulf was stuck in self-destruct mode, and he didn't know where to go with it. The shrink Zander hired for him had told him to find positive ways to spin these moments. For now, all he could think to do was to keep doing the tasks no one else considered, but that would make life easier for those who could help.

Wulf had already picked up Marshall and taken him to Dante. That was who had the best chance of saving him. Now

SPECIALIST

Wulf sat at Beau's house, trying to think of what to say. Finally, he just leaped from the van and headed for the door. He would figure things out as he went.

Beau had a nice house for a single guy who managed a pool cleaning service. But there were a lot of pools in Florida, and he worked for his brother. Wulf imagined Marshall took good care of him. Begrudgingly, Wulf had to admit Marshall seemed to be that guy. He wished now he hadn't given Marshall such a hard time. Wulf hoped Marshall would nurse Dante back to health and Wulf would get his chance to apologize. If not, Wulf feared what he might do.

Wulf followed a stone pathway to the front door. Gorgeous landscaping hid the door from sight. While it probably felt like a fairytale hideaway for Beau, he was dumb. Anyone could break in without being seen by neighbors or anyone driving past. Wulf didn't hold back when he reached the door. It was three in the morning. He knew he had to knock hard enough to be heard. It took a solid five minutes of banging before the door flew open and he found a gun inches from his face. Wulf easily snagged the weapon, disarming Beau without harming him.

"Your brother won't be at work for a while. You'll have to step up."

Beau's hair stood in every direction. He looked sleep-mussed and disgruntled. "What the fuck?" Beau rubbed his forehead. "You woke me up to tell me that?" He hesitated. "Wait. What happened to Marshall? What did you do to him?"

Wulf's throat swelled. It was his fault. Everyone knew he was a bad person without even getting to know him. It was like it was written on his forehead. "It's

Dante. Not Marshall. He got hurt. Marshall..." Wulf couldn't say another word. His throat stopped working, choking off all sound.

Beau's gaze moved over Wulf's face and down his body, as if just now taking in how bad Wulf looked. He had finally remembered to remove his blood-soaked gear, but he still had dried blood on his hands. Wulf couldn't imagine how he looked to someone like Beau. Beau was just a regular guy. He didn't know about the ugliness that surrounded him on every side every second of the day.

"Come inside. I'll make you breakfast."

Wulf shook his head. He invaded Beau's space and tucked the gun in the back of the jeans Beau had obviously hastily donned. Too late, he realized he had his arms around Beau and Beau had a truly amazing body. He was shirtless and his six-pack couldn't be missed. Wulf didn't doubt Beau was one of those single guys who partied all weekend and cared too much about his looks. If only because he had to compete with guys ten years younger than him for attention. He had Wulf's attention, and that wasn't a good thing with Wulf's head where it was at. This was what Wulf did, though, when he was in a bad place. He self-destructed and took everyone with him.

He took a step back. "Sorry. I didn't mean to scare you."

Beau's hand landed on Wulf's chest, stopping him. "Stay."

"No. I—"

"Stay," Beau repeated.

That was a terrible idea. One that could lead to a thousand more awful decisions. Yet Wulf gave Beau a jerky nod and moved closer, leaving the safety of outdoors behind. He already had regrets. But Wulf had a million of those under his belt already and there was no going back now. So he stayed. After all, he had to stop running somewhere. It may as well be here.

A small child in a dinosaur mask crawled into the room, pushing a triceratops across the floor as he went. Rhett crawled in behind him, wearing a matching mask while pushing a T-Rex across the floor. They didn't make any noise, but Marshall couldn't look anywhere else. They had moved Dante to a different room three days ago. It was still a hospital-style room, but it was quieter. A crazy number of people came and went through the place. This room didn't get as much traffic. He gathered through various overheard conversations they were inside Corey and Rhett's home, but the place had a private medical wing. Marshall didn't ask many questions. In fact, he didn't really talk to anyone. He lived in a haze of surreality just waiting for Dante to wake. Nothing and no one else mattered to him.

Rhett's son, Rhorey, kept moving deeper into the room. Marshall winced at the idea of Rhorey playing on this floor. He shuddered at the thought of things this floor had seen. Marshall kept his thoughts to himself. Parents never wanted to hear advice from other parents. Plus, it really wasn't his business. Then Rhorey sat at his feet with his dinosaur and Marshall couldn't ignore him.

"Hi. What do you have there?"

Rhorey pushed up his mask and rubbed his nose before holding up the dinosaur. "It's a triceratops."

He spoke so ridiculously clear—like an adult. It took Marshall by surprise. He had beautiful blue eyes. Marshall couldn't help but smile. "You seem very smart."

Rhorey pointed the dino at Rhett. "I go to school with Dada."

Rhett pushed his mask up and smiled. "I homeschool. We're learning about dinosaurs this week."

Rhorey stood and moved closer to Dante. He went up on the tips of his toes and kissed Dante's arm before dropping back onto the floor with Rhett.

"He wanted to check on Dante," Rhett explained.

Marshall nodded and met Rhorey's stare. "He's still sleeping."

Rhorey rubbed his nose and climbed into Rhett's lap. He kept his gaze locked on his toy as he spoke. "Dante always visited me when I slept here, and now, I visit him so he'll wake up like I did."

His claim confused Marshall. "You slept in here?"

Rhorey pulled his shirt up unexpectedly and showed the nasty scars littering his torso. He didn't say anything.

Marshall's gaze shot to Rhett.

Rhett wrapped both arms around Rhorey and squeezed him against his chest. "Rhorey is one of the kids saved by Dante's team."

Marshall took a breath. He had been on the verge of tears since he got here four days ago, and everything threatened to send him over the edge. "I'm glad he found you."

Rhett smiled and kissed Rhorey's head before setting him free. Rhorey crawled away and used a nearby chair as a mountain for his triceratops to climb. Rhett followed him across the room.

"Every time I see Rhorey, I wonder if he knows yet how lucky he is."

Marshall's gaze shot to the bed.

Dante's eyes were open and shone brightly with pain. His gaze was locked on where Rhett sat on the floor, playing with Rhorey. Dante licked his lips. His voice sounded like his throat had been ripped to shreds. Marshall covered his mouth. Tears threatened to overwhelm him.

Dante still didn't look his way. "I was so much older than him before anyone saved me. I hope he turns out better than me." A tear slid from the corner of Dante's eye, shocking the hell out of Marshall. Marshall had seen this same side of Dante when he had been down with the flu. Under normal circumstances, Dante was cocky to the point of obnoxious. Marshall loved both sides of him, but he couldn't let Dante think he was anything other than what he was: perfect.

"There's no one better than you."

Dante's gaze finally moved Marshall's way. "Since we're at Corey's, I guess that means you know all about me now."

Confusion had Marshall's forehead furrowing. "I've always known all about you."

Dante blinked, as if he wasn't awake enough for this conversation or his brain wasn't quite working completely yet. "How?"

A smile snapped to Marshall's lips. "You told me. When I took care of you while you had the flu, you told me everything about yourself."

Dante looked away.

Worry clenched Marshall's gut. He rubbed Dante's arm. "Do you remember what happened? Do you know why you're here?"

Dante took a ragged breath. It sounded like it hurt. "I'm sorry. I know you didn't want this. You don't have to stay."

Marshall couldn't decide if Dante was still out of it and didn't know what he was saying or what. He hadn't known what to expect when Dante woke, but this weirdness wasn't it. Marshall glanced behind him to see if Rhett thought this was strange too, but Rhorey and Rhett were gone. He looked Dante's way again. "What are you talking about? I mean, of course, I didn't want you to get shot, but why would I leave?"

Dante met his stare. "I know you don't want to take care of anyone else. It's supposed to be your time to play the field and enjoy the freedom you never had. I never meant to tie you down and become a burden. I can't feel my body. You don't want this burden."

Marshall stood and took Dante's hand. "Stop, baby. You're not a burden and I'm not going anywhere. Corey has your muscles deadened to control your blood pressure. It was spiking all over the place yesterday. You're also full of pain meds. That's probably another reason why you can't feel anything. I promise you're not paralyzed."

SPECIALIST

Dante kept blinking, as if fighting tears. "I don't know what's happening."

Marshall bent and pressed his lips to Dante's cheek, trying to keep him calm. "Shhh. You're okay. I'm here. You were shot and damaged a lung, but you made it. Everything is going to be all right. I promise."

More tears poured from Dante's eyes. "I wanted to be the person who took care of you. You deserve better. I never wanted to be a burden to you. I'm so sorry. You need me to be better. I wanted to be your caretaker."

"Please stop. You do take care of me. In fact, you do too much. You don't give me a chance to spoil you as much as I want."

Dante's gaze seemed to finally focus. He held Marshall's stare. "I bought you a ring. I planned to ask you to marry me.

It's okay if you say no, though. We don't even know if Terry will like me yet."

"How could she not like you when I love you this much? I've been so scared waiting for you to wake up." Marshall's voice shook. He couldn't catch his breath. "You can't ever leave me. I think it would kill me. Please don't ever try to send me away again."

The more Marshall broke down, the stronger Dante looked. Marshall realized something. They made each other better. Somehow, they shored up each other's weak spots. They were so much stronger together than they ever would be apart.

"I love you, baby. Stop worrying. I'm not going anywhere. Even if you have to push me around in a wheelchair for a few months, you can rest assured I'll still make you scream at night."

A smile exploded across Marshall's lips. He pressed a quick kiss on Dante's lips. "Ask me whenever you're ready. The answer will be yes. No matter when you ask, it'll be yes."

"Rhorey says he woke you up the way they do in fairytales."

Marshall straightened as Corey came through the door. A laugh burst from him as he realized Rhorey was right. He had. "He really did. Dante woke up right after Rhorey kissed his arm."

Corey smiled as he unwound his stethoscope from his neck. "Kisses are magic." He focused on Dante. "We have to stop seeing each other like this. How are you feeling?"

Dante's gaze kept slipping away from Corey to stare at Marshall, as if he couldn't look at anyone else for too long. "I've been better, but I've also been worse."

Corey nodded as he listened to Dante's heart and lungs. "Don't worry. You'll be back on your feet in no time."

Dante held Marshall's stare. "I know I will. I have too much to do to stay down for too long."

Marshall rubbed his leg. He couldn't move away, even to let Corey do his job. Corey fell into an explanation of Dante's surgery and what his limitations would be now. Marshall stared hard at Dante and silently thanked any god listening for keeping him alive. Even though he knew Dante would eventually make a full recovery, he was still willing to push Dante around in a wheelchair for the rest of his life, as long as they were together. He had never been more grateful for all the times his prayers had gone ignored during the years he thought he would go insane from the loneliness. Marshall realized now he had been waiting his whole life for Dante. He would never give up on them. When Dante gave him that ring, he would scream yes at the top of his lungs. Dante belonged to him. He was never leaving Marshall's sight again. Marshall couldn't go through this again. They were about to be joined at the hip for life. No going back. This was forever.

Chapter Nine

DECEMBER 16TH, MARSHALL'S BIRTHDAY...

Despite having never met Terry, Dante had always been bold as hell. Today, he called on all of that ingrained bravery. In the years since he had been rescued by one of Zander's teams, Dante had learned a lot about himself. He possessed something powerful that won more people over than being nice. He was cocky and people found that irresistible. Dante decided Terry would too if it was the last thing he did. Still, he wiped his sweaty palms on his jeans as he waited for his knock to be answered. Too late, he realized a young woman, living on her own in California, might not answer the door to a stranger. He was more than a little surprised when the door opened.

"Yes?"

She looked exactly like the pictures littering Marshall's home. Red hair she got from her grandmother. Amber eyes like her dad. Dante donned his wickedest smile because he needed confidence to pull him through. "Hey. I'm Dante."

Terry's eyes widened. "*The* Dante? The one dating my dad?"

Dante made a helpless gesture. "The one and only. Well, I had better be the one and only. Otherwise, your dad and I have a problem."

She laughed.

Dante saw it as a win. "I need your help."

A line appeared between her eyebrows. "What's wrong? And why are you here? In California, I mean," she clarified. "Is Dad with you?" She looked past him, as if expecting her dad to pop around the corner any second.

Dante tried answering her questions in order. "Nothing is wrong. I'm here to ask a favor and he's with me, but not right now."

Her confused expression didn't clear. "Okay. What's up?"

"I'm going to ask your dad to marry me."

Her mouth fell open. "No way. Really? That's..." She stared into space for a moment, as if she couldn't think of a way to finish. Finally, she looked thoughtful and smiled. "That's pretty awesome, actually. Dad has been alone for way too long. He needs someone to take care of him. How can I help?"

"I'd like you to be there."

Terry didn't let him down. "Of course. Just tell me when and where."

A smile that felt evil even to him stretched Dante's lips. "Now, if you can."

"Oh." Terry blinked and then glanced behind her. "Um. Okay. Hold on. Hey, babe. Hand me my purse. I have something I need to do."

A blond girl covered in tattoos appeared in the doorway with a handbag. She passed it Terry's way before pressing a quick kiss to Terry's lips. "Be careful. You don't know this guy."

Dante did his best to look innocent. "I swear I'm exactly who I say I am. You can see my license, if you want."

She looked skeptical but didn't respond. Dante could tell she was definitely the more street smart of the two.

Terry rubbed the girl's arm. "It's fine, really. I've heard his voice a dozen times on the phone. I know it's him, but you can always track my phone if you're worried."

She nodded. "I trust your judgment." She gave Terry another quick kiss before she let Terry step outside with Dante. Once they were free, Dante escorted Terry to his car and opened the door for her. They didn't speak again until they were on the road.

"So, does your dad know about that?"

A musical burst of laughter filled the car. "You haven't even married my dad yet and you already sound like him."

A hint of horror hit Dante. She was right. They had just officially met, and he already felt protective of her—like a parent. "Cringe."

Another laugh filled the car, then Terry released a loud sigh. "As it happens, though, no. No one back in Florida knows yet, especially my mom. She'll likely die. I don't know if Dad told you, but Mom holds a lot of bitterness toward gay people. She thinks Dad was lured to the dark side, or some bullshit like that, and ruined all her plans of marrying the hottest guy in town. When she finds out about Anna, she'll probably stop helping with my tuition if I don't agree to just stop being who I am."

Dante was fascinated. Marshall never talked about Terry's mom. He imagined Marshall thought it was bad taste or whatever, but he was engrossed. Still, he couldn't let Terry worry. "Don't worry about tuition. I've got you, if no one else does. Is Anna why you moved to the other side of the country?"

"How exactly do you have the money to make promises like that? Do you sell drugs?"

Dante flashed her a cocky smile. "Your dad didn't tell you he got himself a sugar baby, huh? I have a good job."

The way Terry smiled like she held back laughter had Dante feeling pretty good about how things were going. "That's good to know. That'll stop Beau from treating you like a gold digger when—in fact—it's him you have to watch around Dad's money. As to your question, yes. I met Anna on my senior trip. Thankfully, I had the grades to get into a school here and grab a few scholarships to justify my moving. If not, I would have anyway, but thankfully, I haven't had to face the firing squad yet."

While staring at the road, Dante nodded and mulled over her problem. "Well, if nothing else, you have me and you know your dad won't care. Also, if it makes you feel better, I spend part of my time working here in Cali, so you'll get to see your dad more often."

"Seriously?" The excitement in her voice couldn't be missed. "That's fantastic. You know Dad and I have always been close, but it hasn't really felt that way since I moved. That's on me, obviously. It's hard keeping secrets."

That was one sentiment Dante fully understood. He might have asked Marshall to marry him after a month of dating, if he hadn't thought he kept an entire side of his life hidden. Of course, now Dante knew Marshall was even more amazing than he ever suspected. Marshall had known Dante's every secret from the beginning, and none of it mattered. Their love eclipsed everything. Now Dante had to convince Marshall to marry him as quickly as possible. He couldn't chance ever losing him. Even though Marshall had told him he would say yes whenever Dante asked, Dante still wasn't sure that was true. That promise had been made under duress. There had still been a chance Dante might die at that point. Now that Marshall had time to think and realize he would be trapped with Dante forever, he might not feel the same.

Terry startled beside him. "Shit. Do you mind if we make a quick stop on the way? I promised Dad, when he finally made it to California, I would bring him a bottle of wine from this winery I've fallen in love with since moving here.

It's just up here on the right. Can we stop?"

Dante glanced Terry's way with his eyebrows raised. "Are you trying to get your dad to murder me? How are you buying wine?"

An adorable snort burst from Terry. "Don't worry. It's just wine. A lot of people drink wine with their meals, even teenagers. Scandalous, I know. Dad knows I'm not twelve. Anna works at the winery. Her friend will vouch that it's for Anna, and anyone there will sell to me."

This sounded like a horrible idea, but he wanted Terry to like him, so he followed her directions. The winery turned out to be one he had seen a million times. It was located right next to a wedding chapel. He knew several people who had gotten married there for the backdrop of a beautiful vineyard.

"I'll be right back." Terry jumped from the car.

Dante's nerves ratcheted up by the second. He swiped his palms on his jeans. What if Marshall said no? Dante wouldn't survive it. Terry appeared at his window, startling him from his roiling thoughts. He rolled it down, smiling like the idiot he was. "They wouldn't sell to you, huh?"

Terry's eyes danced with laughter. "Actually, there's a girl working I've never seen, so I didn't try." She bit her lip, looking guilty.

With a sigh, Dante killed the engine and climbed from the car. It wasn't like he was buying wine for an underage girl. Technically, it was a gift for Marshall. There was no reason to feel guilty.

Dante knew something wasn't right the moment he stepped inside. He spotted

Zander and Beau. Then Wulf came into view. Dante's brain went fuzzy as he tried to put the pieces together of why everyone he knew was inside a winery in California. Terry grabbed his arm before he had time to puzzle it out. She dragged him through a door and into the sunshine, where wine grapes littered the land as far as the eye could see. Marshall waited for him.

"What the hell?"

Even Dante heard the confusion in his voice.

Marshall wore a huge grin as Terry led Dante to him. As Dante reached Marshall, Marshall dropped to one knee. Dante's jaw tried hitting his chest. Not once in his life had he reacted so strongly. No one ever got the drop on him.

"Dante Wrath, you are everything to me and I would be honored if you would agree to marry me." Marshall's smile somehow grew. "Today, actually, while all our family is here to witness our love."

Dante covered his mouth. He couldn't believe it. Everything he had planned paled in comparison. "How did you do this?" Dante's voice came out in a whisper. He was closer to crying than he cared to admit. This was the type of surprise that was only for him that he had always dreamed of having.

"I'm on one knee and I'm old."

Dante jumped. "Oh. Yes. Of course, yes."

Marshall shifted to his feet and claimed Dante's lips. When he pulled away, Dante stared in awe as Marshall slipped a band of diamonds on Dante's finger. Marshall's amber gaze lifted and met Dante's stare. "I overheard you on the phone, telling Wulf your plan to surprise me. Terry and I have been plotting against you for weeks. Zander helped a lot."

Dante shook his head. He couldn't believe this was real. "I love you so much."

"I love you too."

As Marshall held Dante's stare, the sheer magnitude of how his life had changed since meeting this man overcame him. He was supposed to be a one-night stand. Marshall wasn't supposed to matter at all. Hell, Dante wasn't supposed to mean anything to Marshall either. Yet here they were in front of their friends and Marshall's family, ready to vow to love each other for the rest of their lives. Life was ridiculously funny. Dante wouldn't have it any other way.

"Are you sure you're ready to spend your life with me?"

Dante couldn't stop smiling. "I must be, since I've never been this happy." And damned if he hadn't smiled like an idiot since the day they met. They were absolutely meant to be.

Keep an eye out for the next Kings of the East, *Hazardous.*

Please consider leaving a review at the retailer where you purchased this book. Reviews really help with a book's visibility, which allows me to continue writing more stories. Thank you, Charity.

About the Author

CHARITY PARKERSON IS AN award-winning and multi-published author with several companies. Born with no filter from her brain to her mouth, she decided to take this odd quirk and insert it in her characters.

*Eight-time Readers' Favorite Award Winner

*2015 Passionate Plume Award Finalist

*2013 Reviewers' Choice Award Winner

CHARITY PARKERSON

*2012 ARRA Finalist for Favorite Paranormal Romance

*Five-time winner of The Mistress of the Darkpath

Connect with her online:

*Sign up for her newsletter: https://sendfox.com/charityparkerson

*Join her readers' group on Facebook: http://bit.ly/CharitysTribe

*Website: https://www.charityparkerson.com

*A list of her social media accounts and giveaways all in one place: http://hy.page/charityparkerson

Content

CONTENT WARNING: THIS SERIES is darker than my usual writing. Since these books bring back Zander and his fight against child trafficking, the deal in kidnapping, sex trafficking (along with everything entailed in that), suicide, and murder. A lot of these characters survived the worst things imaginable and now live with the scars. But now they fight to save people like them.